TERROR ON FLAT TOP RIDGE

A TERRENCE CORCORAN WESTERN

JOHNNY GUNN

WOLFPACK
PUBLISHING
— EST 2013 —

Terror on Flat Top Ridge
A Terrence Corcoran Western

Johnny Gunn

Print Edition
Copyright © 2018 Johnny Gunn

Wolfpack Publishing
6032 Wheat Penny Avenue
Las Vegas, NV 89122

ISBN: 978-1-64119-221-7

TERROR ON FLAT TOP RIDGE

CHAPTER 1

IT WAS A GORGEOUS EARLY FALL DAY WHEN BELMONT TOWN marshal Mason Tetford rambled out of the office and onto the main street, stretching the previous night's activities from his long frame. "A good mornin' to you, Mr. Ahern," he said to the banker who was hurrying up onto the sun-dried boardwalk. "Bit of a hurry are you this morning? How're them peaches coming along?"

Sherman Ahern was not quite forty years old, young to own a bank. His family back in Boston had sent him west to get him out of their hair. He used family money to establish the Belmont National Bank and it was a success from the day he opened the doors. He spent a great deal of time developing a peach orchard in this high-desert climate, and it was described as a total failure in many ways; none of which slowed the banker's efforts.

"Can't say we'll be eating peaches this year, Mase. Late frost… hell man, late deep freeze about ruined this year's crop. What's on my mind this morning, though, is old man Moss."

"What's Bill Moss done now, Mr. Ahern?"

William T. Moss ran a huge cattle and horse operation at

the north end of the Monitor Valley, with as many as ten sections of open rangeland under his control. He raised and trained horses for the army, and supplied a lot of beef for northern Nye County, Eureka, and Austin, even trailing some north to the railhead in Beowawe.

Bill Moss had lost his wife in a tragic horse accident and was raising a son and daughter with help from a Paiute woman nanny, who may or may not offer other household pleasantries, of a more personal nature.

"Fool is behind on his mortgage payments again and is so cavalier about the problem. I lend him the money he needs late every winter and by this time of the year he's supposed to have it paid back. He makes more than enough from his cattle and horses, and I know the army has already picked up their remounts."

For being as young as he was, Ahern was as querulous as a geezer, and seemed to demand absolute perfection from those around him, despite his own obvious imperfections. "I can't abide a man who won't keep his word, Marshal. I'm more than positive that the army paid the ranchers and Moss is holding out on me. I keep my obligations, Sir."

The fact was the army had gathered their horses and paid off the ranchers just two days ago. The fact that Moss hadn't seen fit to rush to the Belmont bank with his gold had the little twit in a twit and Marshal Tetford wanted to laugh right out loud at him.

"Well, I shouldn't be bothering you with this nonsense. Have a good day, Marshal," Ahern said, tipping his hat. He double-timed it down the main street toward the San Francisco Restaurant for his breakfast of toast and tea. Once a Boston gentleman always a Boston gentleman.

Tetford and one other set of eyes watched as Bill Moss and two riders' came into town and tied-off in front of the restaurant. "This might be fun to watch," he murmured and strode to the restaurant with a wry grin on his face.

Tetford was born in El Paso about thirty years earlier and had drifted into being a lawman when he tried to steal an apple pie from the sheriff's wife, who had it cooling on a window sill. He remembered telling a friend about that.

"That man told me he would whup me black and blue, pour molasses over my naked body, and drive me through busted cotton bales with a pick ax if I ever did anything against the law again. The fact that he was my uncle, and my father was his deputy, made me understand I'd just received a great truth in this adventure called life.

"I've carried a badge since I turned fifteen and daddy was killed by that crazy Mexican horse thief, Pedro Gonzalez. He called himself Chapo and my uncle gave me my first deputy badge. Chapo was my first kill, too."

Young as he was, Tetford had a reputation around Nevada and Utah as fast to anger, fast to draw, and held little regard for an outlaw's life. He came north from El Paso through the New Mexico and Arizona territories, even spending some time keeping order in California.

Tetford settled in Belmont, the Nye County seat when their previous marshal was shot up by bandits roaming up from the southern Utah battles with Indians and cattle ranchers. Belmont was home to ranches, mines and mills, and far from any other communities of note. The mining town of Austin was near a hundred miles northwest and the ranching community of Eureka was about a hundred miles northeast.

BELMONT, Nevada was not your typical Nevada mining town/county seat. Sure, there were mines and mills, miners and millwrights, but the difference lay in the fact that

Belmont was also central to a thriving ranching community that spread out across the length of the Monitor Valley. Several large cattle and horse ranches lay in the Monitor cradle with the Toquima Range to the west and the Monitor Range to the east, both ranges offering peaks over eleven thousand feet, which in turn provided considerable water to the valley.

Those vast mountain ranges also provided places to hide, to drive rustled cattle, and was home to elk, mule deer, and antelope which found their way to many a supper table. There were constant fights in the corrals, saloons, boardwalks, and stables between young hot heads. Some called themselves cowboys, some called themselves miners, and all knew they were the toughest.

Marshal Tetford did everything he could to prove to each of them that he was the toughest. More than one cowboy returned to the ranch, and miner to the mine, with knots on his head, teeth missing, and bruises everywhere. Tetford took guff from no one.

In the early days of the community, fights over water rights had been vicious but limited to the immediate area of mines and mills. Fights today were between cowboys and miners over women, poker hands, and status, the same as any other frontier village from the Hudson River to the Pacific Ocean.

"THERE YOU ARE, SHERM," Moss said walking up to Sherman Ahern's table and plopping down in a chair. "Army finally came through with their money." He set a large leather pouch on the table. "This should cover my mortgage and more. Put the leftover on my account. I've always paid my debts, Ahern. I don't appreciate that nasty little note you sent home with my son Jeremy."

Moss's eyes narrowed, his chin jutted some, and Ahern couldn't help but notice that the man was at least twice his size. Sitting in his office surrounded by oak, walnut, and maple furnishings, Ahern was a gruff banker who felt fully justified in sending a blunt note on a past due mortgage payment. All that bluster disappeared when someone like Bill Moss confronted him in a café.

"You've got a lot of nerve, buster," Moss continued. "When my herds sell I pay my bills and you know it. There's a new bank opened in Eureka, Ahern. You want my business, you better get your manners back. You're a rude man, sir. Good day," Moss said loud enough for most of the patrons of the big restaurant to hear.

Bill Moss was gruff with everyone; his ranch hands, his children, his late wife, and at the same time was a teddy bear if someone was hurt or sick. The range was open in the Monitor Valley and the ranchers ran their herds wide open. Branding and ear tagging was essential, and more than one rancher tried to use some runnin' iron of other's cattle. Moss's B Bar M was hard to alter, but there were a few graves filled with those who'd tried.

As hard as he was on them from time to time, his children came first at the Moss spread. Young Jeanne was sixteen and her brother Jeremy was eighteen. Jeremy suffered a terrible childhood, sickly and always small for his age, he never grew into any kind of strength, either.

Jeanne, on the other hand, was tall and scrappy, and absolutely the most beautiful young lady in the Monitor Valley. She could ride the rankest colt, rope the rangiest steers as well as any hand, and still stop a grown man dead in his tracks with her smile.

Moss turned to the men with him. "When we get back to the ranch, you boys gather the rest of the boys and head into the mountains. Bring the herds down for the winter. I'm bettin' on early snow this year." He and his two cowboys walked out the door, mounted their ponies and rode out of town in a cloud of dust.

Mason Tetford had to chuckle watching it all, ordered a rasher of bacon, three eggs, and a platter of biscuits and gravy. "Don't be cookin' those eggs to death, Suzie, and put lots of sausage in the gravy. I'm hungry."

"Don't know why," she smiled. "You ate two steaks and a pot of potatoes and gravy last night." The long rangy marshal just smiled, sipping his coffee.

"BUFORD, get your butt over here, right now." Humboldt Charley yelled at Buford Gamble who was tying off his horse. Charley was sitting near a fire drinking his breakfast from a whiskey flask. "You got any word on that army money? You said you'd know today." Charley was half Paiute and half Louisiana Cajun, and a full-time, angry man. There were many in Nevada who were sure that Humboldt Charley was also insane.

"Army picked up the horses two days ago, Charley," Buford Gamble said stepping off his well-lathered horse. "Moss brought the money into Belmont this morning. Two other ranchers, Slocum and Peabody, brought their money in yesterday. Army paid everyone in gold not script."

Indian wars were raging in the plains, Rocky Mountains, northern Nevada, and elsewhere in the west and the army was buying every horse they could get their hands on. Ranchers like Bill Moss were breeding their herd mares every year and the army continued to demand more.

Buford Gamble was a Texan, wanted just about everywhere in the west, mostly for his excellent knife work. He stood close to six feet and weighed about two hundred and fifty pounds. He carried a sawed off ten- gauge shotgun as a saddle gun and a long- barreled Colt as a sidearm. He usually carried at least two knives. He'd tangled up with Humboldt Charley several months ago.

Humboldt Charley was squat in comparison but deadlier than Gamble. Charley simply did not have respect for any man, woman, or child, and felt no compassion for life itself. Guns were tools and tools were meant to be used, efficiently. No one knew what would make Charley angry and he was known to laugh at a joke and kill the teller of that same joke, too.

"Let's ride," Humboldt Charley said, kicking the fire about. They were camped about three miles outside Belmont along what was called Silver Creek. It would be an easy ride into the bustling little town. "Buford, you stand outside with that scatter gun and the rest of us will take the gold. We'll ride north after we hit the bank."

Humboldt Charley and his gang had been terrorizing areas of Nevada and Utah for some time; robbing banks, rustling herds, and killing anyone attempting to end their actions. The lives of at least three lawmen had been lost along with five or more members of thrown-together posses. From the Green River through Salt Lake into Elko and as far west as Reno, wanted posters of the gang were plentiful.

In this vast area of the west known as the Great Basin, ranches were immense, measured in tens of sections and unfenced. Villages and communities were separated by distances measured in days, and outlaws had no trouble finding safe places to hole up.

Wells Fargo was offering large amounts of gold. The railroad had detectives riding every train passing through, and various county sheriffs and town marshals were ready to kill the gang on sight.

What wasn't plentiful in most of Nevada were people or villages. Most of northern Nevada and northwestern Utah was uninhabited, and Charley and his gang could just melt into the high mountain ranges or the flat desert with ease. High mountains flanked lush valleys, snowmelt and spring-fed trout infested streams, and there was game enough to keep the little gang in food. It would take some doing to catch this band of brigands.

Charley himself was the meanest of the bunch. Gamble a close second, followed by Spittin' Sam Anson out of Waco, Texas. Anson was more than good with his guns, one of which he carried in a holster and the other simply tucked into his waistband. He was fast and deadly. Psychotic would be the best way to describe his personality, which made him more than just dangerous. You never knew what it would be that would bring incensed anger and lingering death.

It was said that Spittin' Sam Anson shot a man in the stomach one night in a saloon somewhere in southern New Mexico Territory just to watch him slowly die a painful and horrible death.

"Kill him, Sam," someone yelled, and Sam said, "No, I want to watch this man die hard." Most agreed that Anson didn't weight a hundred twenty-five pounds after a big supper.

After a few snorts around a campfire, he'd throw the bottle in the air and shoot it, showering everyone with broken glass and daring someone to challenge the act. George Oliver was a bank robber out of California and Enos Payson came west from New Orleans. Some believe that Payson and Humboldt Charley might be related, somehow.

Oliver loved women, drank more than any of the gang, and Humboldt Charley had threatened to kill him more than once. "I might have to grab a woman before we hightail it out of town," he said, taking a drink from his flask. "Ain't had a woman since that little floozie in Austin."

"Put that damn bottle away, you fool," Charley snapped.

"This is gonna be the biggest hit we've ever had, and you better not screw it up, Oliver." Charley then took a drink from his own flask, snickering about it as he did.

"That bank might be so loaded with gold right now that we'll have to steal a pack train of mules to carry it off," Charley laughed, took another long swig from his flask, smiled wickedly at Oliver, and led the gang out of the little canyon and onto the main road to Belmont.

"We'll ride north to the Eureka road and eventually up through the Diamond Valley, boys. I doubt there'll be a posse to come after us, but if there is, George, you and Spittin' Sam hold back and take care of 'em." Spittin' Sam liked that idea, but George was frowning as they loped toward town.

CHAPTER 2

NOBODY PAID MUCH ATTENTION TO THE FIVE MEN RIDING INTO town, after all, cowboys from several ranches were always coming and going, and shift changes at the mines and mills meant people moving about often. Charley led the group right down the main street and they tied their horses off in front of the Belmont National Bank. The bank sat on the east side of the main street.

The Belmont courthouse, an imposing brick structure was off to the west about a block or so and housed all the county offices. Town marshal Tetford had his office on the main floor of the courthouse, tucked away from the county sheriff's large offices, while the district attorney felt more comfortable on the second floor near the district judge's office.

Buford eased out of the saddle, held the scattergun tight to the side of his leg, and stood near the large and heavy front doors of the bank. There wasn't much foot traffic near the bank with most of the action centered a block down the street at the Cosmopolitan Saloon. Charley led the group into the brick and stone building. The men had their bandannas pulled up across their noses and their hats scrunched down low and tight.

Charley, Sam, George, and Enos pulled their weapons and Humboldt Charley barked, "This is a hold up1 Anyone moves wrong or fast, dies." He leaped across the low banister and shoved his revolver into the cashier's face.

Old Moses Peterson had been the bank's front man from day one and had feared a robbery such as this the entire time. His knees buckled when that huge gun was shoved in his face, he gripped the edge of the counter and watched helplessly as the bank seemed to spin slowly around. He was on the floor, unconscious, in two seconds.

Hannibal Wakely stepped out of the vault at that moment and was never closer to death. Charley spun on the movement and almost pulled the trigger.

"Get the gold in these saddlebags, now!" He screamed at the young man and threw five sets of saddlebags across the cashier's cage. A small and aged woman near the cage started to faint and her elderly husband made a grab for her.

Spittin' Sam Anson misread the move and put two heavy chunks of lead in the middle of his chest.

"That'll bring 'em runnin'. Damn it, Sam. Alright, let's move. Get those bags filled." Charley's eyes never slowed down, trying to see everything in every nook and cranny in the bank, every speck of dust, anything that he might consider a threat.

Some at the San Francisco Café looked around at the sound of gunfire, but didn't get too excited. The arrogant young banker scoffed when someone suggested that maybe they were after his gold. He sipped his tea and ignored the riff-raff.

Wakely was stuffing gold coins into the large leather saddlebags as fast as he could, and knew that he might die at any moment. The look on what he could see of Charley's face terrified him. They were the eyes of a madman searching for trouble and had Wakely convinced he would die before they left.

Gamble jerked at the sound of the gunshots and brought the shotgun to the ready, but there didn't seem to be much reaction from those outside the bank. After all, this was a mining town. Underground blasting went on in the various mines day and night. Ugly little barroom disputes ended with wild gunfire sometimes, and unless it was the sound of a bullet passing too close to one's head, well, somebody was just having some fun.

Buford could hear the activity inside and moved to cover the men when they came out at the run. George Oliver and Enos Payson shoved Wakely out of the way and jammed as many gold coins as they could into the bags. "There's more gold than we have room for, Charley," Payson hollered with a giggle in his voice.

"Fill 'em up and let's go. We're runnin' out of time, here." Charley was waving his revolver at two customers and Spittin' Sam was standing near the dead man and his unconscious wife. "Grab those bags and let's go!"

Charley all but screamed. George was dragging three bags and Enos two. Charley grabbed one and Sam another, and they hit the front doors.

Despite the gunshots, no one seemed to be paying attention, but then again, this was a mining town, built right on top of the mines. Steam engines pounded constantly, and it wasn't unusual for a drunk miner or cowboy to fire off a round or two, just for the hell of it.

It took some effort to get the saddlebags on the horses and get mounted. They were at a full gallop and on the way out of town in less than two minutes. "Let's ride hard for a few minutes and then pull back. No need to kill the horses," Charley hollered.

Hannibal Wakely grabbed a shotgun and ran out onto the sidewalk and fired the scattergun to absolutely no effect, the outlaws at least two full blocks away by that time. People slowly made their way out of businesses and homes and toward the bank. Belmont simply didn't have any criminal activity to speak of and a bank robbery in broad daylight didn't enter their minds.

"Were those gunshots?" Tetford asked his chief deputy, Timothy Kleinfelt.

"Sounded like it to me," Kleinfelt answered. He walked over to the door and stepped out onto the broad stone porch of the courthouse. "Maybe near the bank, Mason. Want me to check it out?"

"No, you've got lunch coming. Sit still, I'll walk over." Mason Tetford stepped out onto the street to walk the two blocks up to the bank. He was still a block away when he saw five riders hightail it out of town, and two men running out of the bank yelling at them. When the cashier fired his shotgun, Tetford headed back to the office at a run.

"Damn it," he snarled, grabbed a rifle off the rack, and yelled at Kleinfelt. "Bank robbery. Get a posse together. They're headed north. Catch up to me as fast as you can," Then he jumped on his horse and rode north fast. When he made a sharp turn near the mill and topped the little hill that led out of Belmont, he could see dust several miles ahead of him. He kept his horse in a hard run, but knew he would run out of horse before he could catch up to the robbers.

After ten minutes of hard running, Charley held the group up. "Spittin' Sam, why don't you hold back somewhere around here and kill anyone trying to follow us. Meet us back at that camp near the Moss Ranch. Hand me your saddlebags." He turned the group and led them off at a good trot. It would be a long thirty miles to the Moss Ranch and they wouldn't make it until well after sunset.

Sam Anson wanted to argue about the saddlebags but knew why Charley took them. "I ain't gonna get kilt, Charley, so you keep this gold safe so's I gets my share." Charley just smiled at him and rode off. Sam knew the area where the long north-south road made a wide sweeping turn to the west and then straightened out to run north again. Off to his left he could see the Pine Creek Ranch sitting at the base of the Toquima Range, some five miles off.

Spittin' Sam found an arroyo and led his horse down into the soft sand at the bottom and tied him off to a clump of brush. "That'll keep you out of sight," he murmured and found some heavy sagebrush at the lip of the arroyo where he could hide and wait for whoever might come along. *Charley's still angry about me killin' that old boy but he wouldn't be if that guy had actually been goin' for a gun. He better not be runnin' out on me.*

After several minutes of hard riding, Tetford pulled back to a fast trot and was eating up the miles. The dust from the gang was still visible but when they made the turn around the Eric Thompson ranch at Pine Creek he knew they were gaining on him. He continued to follow hoping that Kleinfelt could get a posse formed and catch up.

Every little canyon from the Toquima Range on the west and the Monitor Range on the east drained into the valley, and during heavy thunderstorms and spring thaw, those creeks ran full. This time of year, many were either barely there or dried-up, and the creek beds, arroyos, were plentiful. Large elk herds came down to winter in the valley and herds of antelope surged up and down the valley.

Tetford brought his horse down to a walk to let him catch his breath and was surprised to hear another horse nicker softly as he neared an arroyo that had carved out some of the valley to his right. He pulled his horse to a stop quickly and started to dismount when a bullet tore into his leg. He toppled to the ground and crawled as quickly as he could into some sage at the side of the road.

His horse stood quietly and Tetford could see his rifle sitting comfortably in its saddle scabbard. "Damn it," he sputtered, pulling his revolver. No other shots had been fired and he hadn't seen who shot him. *Fact is, I didn't hear the damn shot 'till I was halfway to the ground.* Bullets travel a whole lot faster than sound. Hard as he listened, he couldn't hear anything moving. Every nerve ending quivered with anticipation, but there was no sound except his own groans when he moved.

Did someone shoot and run? Not likely. He has got to find out for sure that I'm dead, and that means he needs to come to me. It was a long five minutes before he heard the faintest rustle.

He's comin' up the gulch, The marshal slowly turned his attention from the road to the dry streambed a few yards behind him. Just the barest sound of boots moving through the loose sand and gravel gave Spittin Sam's position away. *I'm gonna see your ugly self in just a minute, piss-ant, and you're gonna die. I don't like people shooting me.*

Tetford was on his belly, his leg aching like it was not only shot but broke too, and he knew that he wasn't going to be conscious for too much longer if he didn't stop the bleeding. *I've got to concentrate on killin' this fool and then stop the bleeding. So, hurry up, fool and make your move.*

Sam knew he had to be close to where the man was, but didn't want to stand up and look over the top of the arroyo and give his position away. Just cuz he shot him didn't mean he was dead. He made his way cautiously, trying to make as little noise as possible. He was listening for any kind of sound but heard nothing and finally knew he had to look. He crept up as close to the side of the gully as he could and peeked carefully over the top. He could see the man's horse but wasn't up high enough to see the road, to make sure the man's body was dead and cold.

Mason Tetford saw a slight movement just to his left and watched as a crumpled hat slowly emerged from the edge of the gully. *Wait. Not yet. Let's see a little more of you, fool. There.* The forty-five barked and the top half of Spittin Sam's head exploded. Tetford slipped the weapon back in its leather, rolled onto his back and sat up, moving so he could lean against a sage. He pulled his scarf, wadded it up, and pressed it hard onto the leg wound.

"Oh, damn, that hurts," he bellowed. He could feel the bones in his leg crunch together when he applied the pressure and wanted to howl, it hurt so much. "What a mess I'm in now," he muttered. He ripped part of his shirttail away and used it to tie the bandanna in place, sweat from the pain dripping across his brow.

He held the bandage in place, could feel the broken bone in his leg, and crawled to his still standing horse. Using a stirrup, he pulled himself up on his good leg and found some leather thongs in his saddlebag. He grabbed the canteen slung over the saddle's horn too.

After a long pull on the water, he let himself back to the ground, and washed off the wound as best he could, and tied off the bandage. He was weak from loss of blood, losing perspective from the onset of shock, and knew he had to get some help if he was going to live. He tried three times to get on his horse but couldn't put any weight on that left leg. Finally, he just slumped to the ground, and held tightly to the reins. *Come on Kleinfelt, I really need you.*

Despite the fact it was early fall, it was a hot day and Tetford passed out more than once as the day wore on. Shock had set in and he would chill to the point of heavy shivering and then find himself in a pool of sweat, even taking his ripped shirt off. His mind was playing tricks as well. He saw riders coming hard, hundreds of them, from the west, he saw winged creatures diving at him, wanting to tear his flesh. He was dying and knew it.

He never heard the posse ride up on him. Kleinfelt leaped from his horse and raced to the marshal's side. "Is he alive?" someone shouted. Kleinfelt could see that Tetford was breathing and nodded.

"He's been shot, and his leg is broke. I can see the bone right through a rip in his pants. Find a limb of some kind and let's get this leg tied off so he can sit on his horse." Kleinfelt used Tetford's canteen to splash some water on the marshal's face and felt him stir a bit. He tilted his head back and dribbled some water into Tetford's mouth.

"There you are, old man. I knew you'd come around."

Mason Tetford opened his eyes and reached for the canteen. He took a long drink and coughed a little before he tried to speak.

"Dead man in the gully over there," he said. "Bastard hid in the bushes and shot me. I never saw anything but his hat, so I don't know who he is."

Jake Willoughby walked up. "Ain't no branches good enough for a splint, Tim. I'm gonna ride up to Thompson's ranch there and get a wagon to take the marshal back to town."

"That'll work good, Jake," Tetford said. "When you get me in the wagon, Kleinfelt, I want you to continue riding north and see if you can figure out where those jaspers are going. I'm gonna be out of the picture now for a while, Tim, so we're really depending on you. Take someone with you.

"Pappy, you up to doing a little tracking?" He was talking to William "Pappy" Somerset, an elderly gentleman who scouted in his early years for the army.

"I might be fifty or so, Marshal, but I can still track a snake. I'll ride with you, Timmy, boy. Doc Hastings will have you on your feet soon, Mason. Just enjoy the ride back to town and leave the rest to me and Kleinfelt."

Tetford knew that Tim Kleinfelt would never find the bank robbers but felt certain that Pappy Somerset would, and would keep the young deputy on the job. "Thanks, Pappy."

It was more than an hour before Eric Thompson showed up with a wagon to take Marshal Tetford back to Belmont. Thompson was grumpy most of the time, lost a couple of water rights court cases to a mining operation near his ranch, and felt those in Belmont supported the mines more than the ranchers. "So, these fools robbed old Sherm Ahern of all his gold, eh? Good for them!" he cackled, watching the posse get Tetford loaded into the wagon. "You're sending Kleinfelt to catch 'em? Hell's bells, boy, they'll be in Winnemucca before he reaches Moss's place."

CHAPTER 3

IT WAS A BEAUTIFUL AFTERNOON AND TERRENCE CORCORAN was slowly walking through heavy sagebrush and rabbit brush, a fine shotgun held lightly at the ready. An explosion of sound and fury blasted from a sage just twenty feet in front of him, he raised the piece and swung hard to the right, pulling the trigger as he did. A large sage grouse folded its wings and nose-dived into the dirt, fluttered for just a moment, and was still.

"Supper, trail snack, and supper again," the big Irishman said. "A man's fowling piece is almost a guarantee to fine dining," he chuckled wiping sweat from his brow after cleaning the large bird. "I've got some potatoes, carrots, and onions, and I think I'm gonna do me a Dutch oven supper."

It was about half a mile back to his camp along what fifty years ago would have been considered a fair beaver creek. Left over dams were still evident, but the critters weren't. He was high in the Monitor Range of central Nevada, camped above the eight- thousand-foot level. It had already snowed above the ten-thousand-foot level, and the water in the creek was cold.

Corcoran was born on the boat just a day or so out of

Dublin, raised on the east coast waterfronts in Irish enclaves and had never given up his Irish romantic soul, humor, or delight in a fine fight. He didn't travel light... almost always with a pack mule and his camp were legendary. "A man should not venture far from home without benefit of cast iron cooking pots," he'd tell anyone wanting to listen.

Corcoran was a big man, tall and rangy. His long reddish hair hanging in waves and curls hadn't seen a pair of shears in many weeks, and he hadn't bothered to shave his rugged face either. Bright green eyes twinkled at the slightest hint of a joke, but he would pull and fire to kill just as quickly. It was the bright eyes and lovely smile that got the women folk all fidgety and he knew how to use that smile.

After his early years on the Boston docks, Terrence Corcoran came west as soon as he was old enough to run away. He was a fast learner, worked his way west on ranches learning everything he could about that life. He knew horses and cattle, carried a badge often, loved to fight almost as much as he loved pretty women, and was a born storyteller.

Corcoran had a strong sense of right and wrong, would not tolerate a woman being mistreated in any way by any man, but was also known to bend the law... just a bit you know, if it became necessary for him to complete a job or sway a lovely lady.

Corcoran had ridden out of Eureka two days earlier, trailing a well-packed mule, and was looking forward to a long week or two high in the mountains, chasing elk, shooting birds, and "swimming naked with the fish."

"You take as much time as you want, Corcoran," Sheriff Fred Seagram had said. Corcoran had ridden into Eureka two weeks before, just to say hello to his old friend, and got tangled up chasing down a group of Paiutes that had been stealing cattle in the Diamond Valley.

"They learned the craft well," he joked- telling the story.

"They took a steer and left a bit of trail to be followed. When those cowhands got riled and on the trail, the main group rode in cool as all get out and took the rest of the herd. They honed that skill bushwhacking the army up the Black Rock Desert.

"They'd pester a wagon train, see, and the army would come and follow that trail right into an ambush. Old Captain Wells got nailed a couple of times. Scarface and Paiute Jack were leading this bunch, sheriff. You gonna give these boys to the army?"

"Yup," the sheriff said. "You did a damn fine job out there, Corcoran, and got yourself busted up besides. How did that happen?"

"I got the story from the cowboys about the herd being rustled. When those boys told me it was Scarface that took the herd, I went on the trail. Been lookin' for that sumbitch for a couple of years now. He and Humboldt Charley are on my to-do list, sheriff." He took a long sip of coffee laced with some good bourbon. "I got on that trail sudden like and found the herd and four Indians holding it.

"The rest were off somewhere, and I didn't scout them out like I should have. That night I took out the four, one at a time, but the fourth one squalled some and brought Scarface and the rest down on me. I emptied my Colt and Winchester, and when I ran out of bullets, we went at it personal-like. It was Scarface that whacked me with that damn club, but he slipped and took my knife across his chest.

"I had to play nurse to the four that I brought you, sheriff. That's why it took a couple of extra days to get back to town."

Fred Seagram took a sip from his coffee followed by a sip from a flask. "Get yourself put back together and come see me. You'll have a job in this department anytime you want it."

Corcoran and Seagram had been friends for many years,

riding from the law and for it, in Texas, Wyoming, and now in Nevada. "It'll be a while before those ribs heal up, Fred," Corcoran said. He mounted his horse slowly, wincing as he swung into the saddle. "That old boy whopped me a good one with that cedar post. Ripped it right out of the ground and swung it like an ax." Seagram was laughing as he watched Corcoran ride west out of Eureka, trailing that well-packed mule.

Four Paiutes pushing some twenty head of stolen cattle and that man took 'em all on. You come back, Terrence Corcoran. Come back and wear a badge with me.

HUMBOLDT CHARLEY LED the gang at a solid trot up the long valley. "Let's not go back to the mountains, boys. Let's ride to the big ranch we passed by a couple of days ago. What did you call that place, Gamble?"

"That's Moss's place, boss. We've got a lot of his gold in these bags," he laughed. "I followed him down the valley to tell you he put it in the bank." Everyone got a good laugh at that.

"How many people around that place?"

"You got something in that head of yours, Charley. What you thinkin' about?"

"Big piece of beef and maybe a woman," Humboldt Charley answered. "Are there lots of hands at this big old Moss ranch?"

"No," Buford Gamble answered. "Most of the hands are up in the hills bringing the herds down for the winter. He's got a woman works for him and a couple of kids. One's a daughter with some good looks." Gamble had a hungry look on his face saying that.

"You got a good idea, Charley," George Oliver hooted, standing tall in the saddle. "A woman and some roast beef.

Hell, I might hold off on eating if there's women around that place."

"You are a dawg, George, but I get first pick and you all better remember that." Charley scowled, waved his rifle about and then roared in laughter watching the men cringe some. "I'll kill any man tries to take a woman I claim," he screeched in mad laughter.

It was quiet for some time after that scene and they made good time riding up the valley, but it was starting to get dark and they hadn't reached the ranch yet. "How much further, Gamble? We've been riding for hours."

"We've got another hour, Charley. Ain't no moon tonight, either."

"See that line of trees out there?" He was pointing at a line of cottonwood trees about a mile off toward the base of the Monitor Range. "Should be good firewood and fresh water. Let's camp there tonight and raid the ranch in the morning. Payson, you hold back after we ride off this trail, and drag some sage to clean our trail. I'm sure there'll be a posse along at some point."

Humboldt Charley had insisted that when they were riding cross-country, they rode single file and the last rider would rip some sagebrush and drag it along behind his horse, wiping out any sign they had ridden through. "Did you learn that from one of your Paiute brothers?" Buford Gamble asked him one time.

"Hell no," Charley said. "An old card shark outside Houston taught me that trick. He dragged cotton plants one time instead of brush and the posse simply followed the tufts of white stuff until they shot him dead."

They were all laughing hard at Charley's story. "I ain't worried so much about our trail in here. What's could give us away will be any fire we get built up. Let's get as far off that main road and as far back into a canyon as we can. Don't need no deputy ruinin' our night."

Humboldt Charley's Paiute mother was working as a hotel maid in Wells and fell in with a Cajun gambling man from New Orleans. When he found out she was pregnant, he took her out to where the town of Wells originally got its name, the Humboldt Wells, a set of springs that are the origin of the Humboldt River.

At the springs, the gambler pulled a knife to kill the woman and discovered the short, squat little lady had a shiv of her own. Charley loves to tell that tale. "That fat old whore killed my father and named me after where she buried his butt." He'd dance around, swinging his knife dangerously at whoever was close, laughing like the fiend he was.

"Where you figure these outlaws are heading, Pappy?" Timothy Kleinfelt was just twenty-two, in his first year as a deputy marshal, and not in the best of physical condition. He ended up as deputy because he was not capable of the hard work in the mines. Mason Tetford had complained about how he would shirk his duties, not be fully reliable, but since he was the nephew of the town's senior council member, Tetford was limited in what he could do about it.

"They'll ride 'till dark and find a place to camp. Figure they'll ride north tomorrow, probably all the way to the Humboldt River. We won't catch 'em tonight, boy, but we'll have a go at 'em tomorrow sometime."

"Tomorrow? You mean we're staying out here tonight? Shouldn't we head back to town?"

"We're chasing a gang of bank robbers who've already proven they're ready to kill, boy. They shot Marshal Tetford, they killed old man Smithson, and they have most of Ahern's gold. We ain't quittin' boy." Pappy Somerset had his jaw set, his shoulders squared, and could almost feel the old uniform wrapped around his bones.

I've rode with some fine generals and they wouldn't allow this boy to polish their boots. What has gone wrong with these young people?

Kleinfelt wanted to say that he was the deputy, it was his posse, and he didn't want to continue the chase. He knew if he said that or tried to do that, that he would no longer be able to live in Belmont, or probably even Nevada. "I'm not gonna quit, Pappy, but we don't have anything with us. Maybe we should go back and get supplied right."

Pappy Somerset ignored the boy and continued at a fair trot easily following the trail of the four outlaws. The sun was fading toward the high peaks of the Toquima Range and he knew it would be getting dark soon. "As long as we can see the trail, we'll ride 'till dark then make camp. Might get lucky and shoot a jack rabbit for supper." Pappy couldn't see Kleinfelt's sour look but smiled figuring it was there.

They ran out of light about half an hour later, moved off the main road, and set up camp near some willows along a dry creek. Pappy popped a rabbit as they rode in and had Kleinfelt do the cleaning chores while he gathered firewood and spread his blanket.

"I ain't never done this."

"Ain't nothin' hard about it, boy. Take out what you don't want to eat, take the skin off, and we'll cook it. Where were you raised, anyway?"

"San Francisco," the young man whispered.

"If we're being followed by someone who can track, they'll see where we left the road last night so let's not give them a good look at where we come back onto the road." Humboldt Charley knew there was trouble when Spittin' Sam hadn't been seen. "We'll ride straight to the ranch and make plans after we've et their food and drank their likker."

"And had some fun with their women," Oliver laughed.

"Whiskey and a warm woman is what I need right now. What are we waitin' for Charley>"

"He's hopin' Spittin' Sam shows up, jackass," Buford Gamble snarled.

"That I am, and if you don't like it, make your play," Humboldt Charley snapped, his big right-hand hovering close to his weapon. Oliver didn't say anything, just turned around and walked toward the horses. All the men realized that even when Humboldt Charley was laughing at a joke he could turn mean and deadly quick as a snake.

Charley spat a wad tobacco juice and snickered, knowing none of his gang would ever challenge his fast draw and deadly aim. Sometimes it was fun to just play with them, sometimes he wanted them all dead or dying. Sometimes the hate boiled and steamed until all he could feel was poison, all he could see was somebody dying.

He waited another ten minutes just to mess with George Oliver and said, "Alright, I guess we've lost ol' Sam. Let's ride for women and likker. We'll fast trot the distance and be able to make a defense at the ranch if we do have followers."

He had already forgotten what Gamble said about returning to the main road and led the gang right on out like it didn't matter if the posse knew they were moving. *Sometimes that man is an idiot and other times a full- bore genius. If there is a posse, we'll have a fight. Shame we lost Spittin' Sam Anson.* Gamble was smiling just a bit knowing there was one less man to share the gold.

They covered the few miles to Moss's place in quick time and rode straight to the main house. It was a two-story affair with gables on all four sides and a covered porch that surrounded the building. Big Bill Moss heard the riders coming in and stood at the open door, a shotgun close to his side but out of sight.

He didn't recognize any of the riders and hadn't put out

the word that he was looking for help. "These boys must have been camped somewhere nearby since it ain't too much past sunrise," he muttered. His son was in the barn and his daughter wasn't even up yet, and the rest of the hands were up in the hills with the herds.

"Mornin'," he said. "You boys lookin' for work, I'll be hirin' in about three or four weeks. You'll have to come back then." There wasn't much friendliness in his tone or his face.

"We're settled, old man. Don't need any of your stinkin' work," Humboldt Charley said, drawing his big iron and killing Moss with two shots before the rancher could budge the shotgun. "Let's see what's for breakfast boys," he said, stepping off his horse.

They didn't bother to move Moss's body from the doorway, just stepped over the bleeding hulk. Charley, Enos Payson, and George Oliver were in the front room of the ranch house looking at a blazing fire in a massive rock fireplace. "No stew pot," Charley snarled.

Jeremy Moss, eighteen, and according to the old man, dumber than an ox and just as strong, came running from the barn holding a pitchfork, still trailing some grass. "What the hell's the shootin'?" he hollered. He made three more steps before Buford Gamble shot him in the leg, toppling the boy, face first, into the dirt.

"I want that kid alive," Gamble snarled, hearing two more weapons being cocked. "He'll tell us where the old man keeps his money." Gamble walked over and kicked the pitchfork away and rolled Jeremy onto his back with his boot toe. "You ain't gonna die. Quit yer blubberin'." He jerked the big kid to his feet getting a scream of pain from him.

Jeanne Moss woke with a start. "What was that?" She was wiping sleep from her eyes when another gunshot went off, and she leaped from bed, grabbing her robe. Jeanne was tall and thin. Her long legs were still little-girl skinny, but the rest of her was fully developed, though still somewhat small. The sixteen-year-old filly had a swell to her bust, and her hips were more than evident despite the robe.

Bill Moss often said Jeanne should have been a boy but any man or boy that looked knew she wasn't. She could ride better than most men, could throw a rope better than Bill, and like her father, took no guff from any man.

She flew from the bedroom and was halfway down the stairs when she saw her father's body crumpled in the door-way. She screamed and raced to him, crying for Jeremy just as Gamble shoved her brother onto the porch. She started to kneel next to her father and was shoved away by George Oliver. "Not for such sweet and pretty eyes," he said, taking advantage of her awkwardness to fondle areas he shouldn't be anywhere near.

"Get your hands off me, you murderer. Get away from me!" Jeanne screamed in his face, wrenched free for a second before Oliver again had her in his clutches. "No!" she screamed again as he let his hands roam some. She was fighting the ugly man, but his strength was far superior. She tried to scratch, kick, even bite, and Oliver just kept trying to hug her close to him.

"Knock it off, Oliver. There's time for that later," Humboldt Charley laughed. He grabbed Jeanne by the arm, twisting her away from Oliver and pushed her onto a large couch sitting near a massive rock fireplace. "That your father lying there?" he asked.

She was shaking in terror and anger, couldn't keep her eyes off her dead father, and hurt from the hard hands of both Oliver and Charley. She nodded without looking at the men, unable to speak. "Take us to the kitchen and fix us food," Charley snarled, jerking her back to her feet. "Gamble, bring that kid in, too. Oliver find the booze and bring it in."

He kept a firm grip on Jeanne's arm as she led them into a

large, warm kitchen where a cast-iron cook stove was already lit, and coffee was boiling. Jeanne was a smart young woman and tried to understand what was happening. Why did these men shoot her father, why did they shoot Jeremy, and why was the horrible man trying to put his hands all over her? She didn't have any answers, but knew she had to figure out some way to get out and find help.

"Breakfast, girl, and make it fast." Charley found a rack filled with large mugs and put four on the table, filling one with coffee. "What's your name, girl?"

"Jeanne," she whispered, adding some wood to the fire-box. "Jeanne Moss. You won't get away with this." Despite her fear, she had her anger up. She stirred the fire, looked at Humboldt Charley. He wore regular canvas pants and a wool shirt, a black leather vest with silver Conchos, and a black hat with a feather in it. *He's the ugliest Indian I've ever seen. Why is this happening?*

"Yes, we will," Humboldt Charley snickered, smacking the girl on her bottom end. "Food can wait," he said, and forced himself on her, right in the middle of the kitchen, and purposely in front of Oliver. Jeanne screamed in pain and fear, bit Humboldt Charley on his neck, and took a brutal fist to the face for the effort. Thankfully, Jeanne Moss was mostly unconscious through the rest of the attack.

Jeremy was wrestled into the ranch house and flung on the floor in front of the fire, listening to his sister's screams of terror. The bullet had torn through his leg breaking the thigh bone and causing incredible muscle damage. He was moaning in pain and unable to help his little sister.

CHAPTER 4

Pappy Somerset watched the sky lightening and kicked young Kleinfelt awake, dumped some more sagebrush on the fire and poured his second cup of coffee. "Get up, kid, it's time to ride."

"The sun's not even up," Kleinfelt whimpered. He hadn't slept outside in more than ten years and his body ached from rolling around on the rocks and brush. Pappy told him how to smooth out the ground before laying his blanket down, but he didn't pay any attention to that nonsense.

He slipped out of his blanket and got his boots on. Somerset handed him a cup of boiling coffee. Fear kept the sleep away much of the night. He feared the snakes would get under the blankets with him, knew the outlaws were coming back to kill him, and damn near wet himself when the first coyote began to sing. All of that and rocks for a mattress. "Ain't no time of the day to be getting' up."

"We're not far from the Moss Ranch, Mister Deputy Town Marshal, and those men we're chasing tried to murder your boss yesterday. I ain't gonna ride with no cry-baby so you better get some tough in you, and I mean right now. Swill that coffee and git saddled."

Neither man spoke another word for the next hour as they rode north toward the Moss place. Kleinfelt was thinking what a terrible mistake it had been for him to go along with his uncle and put on that tin badge. Mason Tetford was a demon, making him learn how to shoot, how to fight, and how to be responsible. Kleinfelt had no idea what life was all about, simply rode it out, day to day.

It wasn't a case of not knowing what to do with his life, it was a case of not knowing that he even had a choice in the matter. Raised in a sophisticated city by parents who had no time for a child. He was privately tutored, his only friends were equally mistreated, and the idea of developing a future that he created never entered his mind. He was sent off during late teen years to an uncle in the wilds of Nevada. Tim Kleinfelt had no concept of life.

Pappy Somerset was thinking what a terrible mistake it had been for him to ride with the kid. *I don't intend to die on this ride and I'm not gonna let this kid get me killed, either. I'll never know why Mason Tetford hired this fool, but I ain't gonna let him get me killed. How many times have I seen wet behind the ears lieutenants lead their units right into a massacre, despite all the efforts of senior non-coms and old-time scouts? Ain't gonna happen today.*

Somerset had been in the Powder River area during that massacre, had guided and tracked for some fine generals and could tell stories of very young lieutenants who cried themselves to sleep at night. "This boy is about the worst, though," he muttered, riding some ten yards or so in front. He pulled his horse up and when Kleinfelt joined him he pointed at the trail.

"See how the trail simply ends?"

"How is that possible?" he asked. "What happened?"

"Listen to me, boy. You're wearing a badge and chasing men who have killed more than one person who wore a badge. You get your head screwed on right or you're gonna be dead before this day is half over." He got off his horse, nodded to Kleinfelt to do the same, and pointed out the little signs in the dirt and sand.

"They rode off the trail to the east, boy. Then one man came back and with some sage or something and brushed the trail clean. It's a fool's trick, cuz it's so damn obvious. In about a half a mile, we'll come onto their tracks again where they rode back onto the trail.

"You understand anything I'm saying?" All the time he was pointing out what it was he was describing, he saw that the young man wasn't really paying much attention. "If you don't learn these things, you ain't gonna live long carrying that badge. Let's ride," he snarled. They mounted and continued north.

As Somerset predicted, about half a mile north they rode up on the tracks of four horses coming onto the main road and he pointed them out to Kleinfelt. "What would you have done, boy, when those tracks just ended back there?" Somerset asked.

"I don't know," the deputy murmured. "I mean, there wouldn't be anything to follow. If you hadn't told me I wouldn't have known what any of that meant. How do you know these tracks are the same ones we were following?"

"You've got to pay attention, boy," Somerset growled. "There are four horses and you've got to look at the shoe and hoof prints. One of the horses is missing a shoe. Another has a very worn set of shoes, which leaves distinctive marks in the dirt. You gonna be trailin' outlaws that want to kill you, you gotta open your eyes and turn on your dumb-ass brain."

Somerset knew that he was letting his anger get away from him, took a deep breath and continued his lessons in how to be a tracker. "Now look at that trail and tell me what you see."

Kleinfelt was not an observer and apparently had never been one. "Well, I see where four horses have come out of the desert and onto the trail. What else would I see?"

"When they came out of the brush and onto the road, the horses were walking. Did you notice that very soon they were moving at a fast trot?"

"Oh," he said. "Yeah, I see that now. Does it matter to us, though?"

"It means, boy, that those outlaws are probably already at the Moss place and we're not. We need to put these horses in an equally fast trot because I'm sure old Bill Moss and his kids are in trouble." He spurred his mount into a good hard trot and Kleinfelt stayed right with him.

"Shouldn't we get help?"

"You got some idea where that might come from?" Somerset said, looking around at the vast openness of the Monitor Valley. "Son, they ain't nobody within thirty miles of where we are. Moss and his family need help and that help is us." He was spittin' mad and needed to blame someone for the boy's worthlessness.

Tetford's had this boy as a deputy for more than a year. He should have taught him all this stuff. Tetford's a well-known gunfighter and he's just coddling this boy. I'm gonna have words with him.

With some help from his sister, Jeremy Moss got the bleeding stopped and a clean bandage wrapped around his leg. "Does it hurt bad, Jere?" she asked. "I'm scared. They killed pa and shot you. What will we do?" Her face was bruised, she was still in her nightgown, what was left of it. She had a robe wrapped around her, but Jeremy could see that she was bleeding and bruised. He could see where she had been hit and feared the worst.

"I don't know, but we gotta get help. Even old Pancake rode out with the crew, and Whispers Soft is back with her

36

people for a week or so." Jeremy wasn't a fast thinker and just sat letting his sister work on his leg. He was in the big chair by the fireplace when Oliver stalked out of the kitchen and grabbed Jeanne by the hair and forced her into the kitchen.

"Let go of her. Let her go," he commanded, and Oliver dropped Jeanne to the floor, took two steps to the big chair and smashed Jeremy in the head, knocking him clear out of the chair. He laughed, grabbed the sobbing Jeanne by the hair and dragged her into the kitchen.

It was slow in coming, but it finally dawned on young Jeremy, lying on the floor bleeding, that he was alone, and he slowly got up and limped out of the large ranch house. That little effort caused the wound to open and the bleeding started again. He hobbled to the tied-off horses, crawled up onto one and rode from the ranch at a full gallop, never looking back.

"What was that?" Humboldt Charley was sitting at the table, a plate of side meat and potatoes half-eaten in front of him. He jumped to his feet just as Oliver was half dragging, half attacking Jeanne near the entryway from the great room to the kitchen. Hearing the horse run away, Oliver pushed off Jeanne, crashed into Charley, and fell to the floor.

"That was a horse," Enos Payson said, getting to his feet as well. He had been nursing a bottle of whiskey instead of eating breakfast, and wasn't that sure of where his feet were going when he stumbled over Jeanne Moss.

Charley got clear and he and Oliver ran to the front door and onto the porch. "It's that kid," Oliver howled, seeing the dust way out on the main road.

"We gotta get out of here," Humboldt Charley said. "He'll stir up a nest of lawmen. Find two horses, Oliver, and I'll get the others. We gotta go now and fast." Oliver ran to the barn to find horses, one for the girl and one to replace the stolen horse, and Charley ran back into the ranch house.

He grabbed Jeanne and smacked her hard across the face. "Where's your father keep the money?"

She whimpered but understood that Jeremy had gotten away. "Probably in his office. You won't find much cuz he went to the bank yesterday." She pointed at a doorway that led to a small room under the broad staircase. Humboldt Charley flung the door open and found a desk, a cabinet with folding doors and opened them. Just shelves.

He opened all the drawers in the desk and found nothing. He didn't look under the throw rug and didn't find the safe. "No time for this," he snarled. "Let's go." He kept a tight grip on Jeanne's arm leading her out and threw her onto the back of a horse. She was still wearing just her bloody nightgown and robe, and way too much of her was exposed. Oliver took the reins and led her horse and the gang rode out and turned north on the main road.

She knew Jeremy was hurt bad, was bleeding heavy and worried that he would not be able to ride all the way to Belmont and bring help. She worried too that she would not live through this ordeal. *These men must be running from something or someone, for them to get this riled when Jeremy ran off. I've got to get away, got to get help.* In her short life she had never been this frightened of anything, and the pain of the attacks was more than just physical. She was humiliated to the core of her soul by the vicious attacks.

Humboldt Charley led them off the road about a mile or so north and turned cross-country toward a hot spring, several miles to the east. They rode past the springs and up into the lowest hills of the Monitor Range. He followed a small creek that still had the remains of a few beaver dams and flowed from a meadow, a thousand-feet or so above the valley floor.

The creek was in a deep canyon that led them higher into the craggy mountains. Great spires of rock lined the canyon, and from time to time they rode across plateaus filled with trees and good grass. There was considerable water flowing in the creek that they forded often in their climb. For millions of years water had cascaded off the Monitor Range, and the canyons that had been carved were rugged.

They rode without stopping for several hours, following that stream higher and higher into the vast mountains. "You know where you're going?" Payson asked, the effects of the bottle of whiskey turning into a serious headache.

"I been here," Charley snarled. They wound through a series of small canyons where spring runoff sent water into the stream, and ended on a plateau filled with grass and a few scraggly trees. It may have been a ridge that, because of erosion, now was almost flat on top. There was good grass, trees were thick in places, and it would be easy to defend. Looking up the mountain one could see that these plateaus were stacked about five hundred to a thousand feet above each other.

"Make us a camp we can defend, Payson. Oliver, you keep your hands off that girl and get some wood. Buford, come with me. We got to do some thinkin' here." The two rode a couple of miles higher into the range and settled under a rock overhang. Humboldt Charley and Buford Gamble tied their horses and squatted into the dirt. "We lost a set of saddlebags filled with gold when that kid rode off. Damn Oliver and women. More interested in that girl than watching the boy."

Charley's eyes were darting about not really seeing anything except the need to kill. He kicked a rock, picked a smaller one up and threw it as far as he could and took two quick shots, hitting it with both. "I'll see his blood flow like that stream and rub his foul face in it," he stormed.

"We need his gun, Charley. Don't be killin' him, yet. Any

good rock fields around here? We need to move fast tomorrow and not leave a good trail."

"Yeah, about ten miles north we can ride into them and get back down the other side of this range. Soon's we get a chance I'm gonna kill that fool. Sure as hell, that boy's gonna bring the law on our tail. We'll leave out at first light."

"You think it's a good idea to bring that girl with us?" Buford had enjoyed his time with her, but he was a practical man. "She's gonna be trouble, gonna slow us down, and as much as I hate to say it, we got to leave her."

"Yeah," Charley said. "Damn fine little filly, though. Oliver will ruin her in no time. We'll leave her." They heard a rifle shot as they rode back toward camp and came in at a gallop.

"What's the shootin?" Charley hollered. He jumped from his horse and had the big revolver in his hand, cocked and ready.

"Payson got us a nice deer for supper," Oliver said. He had the girl's robe off and she was sitting near the fire, hands tied behind her, in just a nightgown. She was crying, and Charley could see scratches across George Oliver's face. Despite the scratches, Oliver was wearing a smile. "She's feisty," he chuckled, "and so damn good. So soft."

Charley still had the gun in his hand and stormed over to Oliver, his face distorted in anger and madness. He swung the large pistol, driving the steel across Oliver's head instead of shooting the man, and heard Jeanne Moss cry out. He spun toward her, pointed the big gun at her, and then howled in laughter. She cringed in terror at his actions, which made Charley laugh even more.

Humboldt Charley stopped laughing and turned to Oliver once again, and back into a fury. "You let that boy escape, Oliver, and with bags full of gold. We may take that little problem out of your share." Humboldt Charley was sneering at the man, challenging him right out. "Now you're telling me that this pretty little girl is more important than us getting out of this alive."

Oliver pushed the girl away and stood facing Charley, his legs slightly spread, his hand hovering just off his sidearm. "You're pushin', Charley. I don't like to be pushed."

"Do something about it," Charley snarled. "You ain't got it in you, Oliver. You ain't gonna draw on me." Charley turned to Buford Gamble. "When we bed down tonight, Gamble, you take the first watch, and Payson, you get the second. Don't let this coward shoot me in the back," and he howled with laughter, raised that big Colt, still cocked, and shoved it in Oliver's face.

"You should have pulled the trigger, Charley," Enos Payson said later. "That man's gonna be the death of us yet."

"I will, Payson, I will." He uncocked the weapon and slid it back in its holster, grabbed Jeanne Moss and dragged her off into the bushes where he untied her legs and attacked the poor girl one more time.

CHAPTER 5

"Rider comin'," Somerset called, pulling his horse off the road and into the sagebrush. He jumped from the saddle, rifle in hand, and waited for the lone rider to come close. Kleinfelt was a little slow but did manage to get into the brush and off his horse. "That's young Jeremy Moss," Somerset said, stepping out onto the road to flag the boy down.

"Mr. Somerset, I'm sure glad to see you," Jeremy said, almost falling out of the saddle. The bandage was dripping blood and Jeremy had little strength left as Pappy Somerset caught him and eased him down onto the roadway.

"Is that a gunshot, boy? Grab that horse, Kleinfelt."

"Four men came to the ranch this morning. They killed pa and shot me, but I escaped. They have Jeanne."

"I was afraid of something like this," Pappy murmured. "Get some water over here, Kleinfelt. We've got to get this wound taken care of right now. You said there were four of them?"

"That's right. This is one of their horses. It was tied off and when I snuck out of the house, I just grabbed it." He was fighting to stay conscious but losing the battle and when

Pappy removed the bandage Jeanne had made, Jeremy passed out from the pain.

"That's a nasty wound. It's better that he's unconscious," Pappy Somerset said. He pulled his knife and told Kleinfelt to get a fire started. "Tie off them horses, too." *Shouldn't have to tell him that, but damn me, I'm glad I did.*

He almost chuckled as he tested the blade and put it back in its leather, and dragged young Moss off the road and into an area free of brush, found a patch of open ground and laid him out. "Gotta get that bullet out or he'll die of infection before the day's out."

Kleinfelt couldn't watch as Somerset probed with his gnarly fingers, finding the bullet up against Jeremy's thighbone. "Hope that bone ain't broke, too," he said. He held the knife in the fire for a minute, getting it hot and hopefully getting the germs burned off.

"Open my saddlebags, boy, and bring me the flask that's in there." He made a deep slit in Jeremy's leg, right across the top of the wound, probed some more, and pulled the bullet free. "Hurry with that whiskey, dammit," he snarled. "Quit bein' so damn slow, deputy. This man's tryin' his best to die on us." He grabbed the flask with one hand, pulled the rags he stuffed in the wound back, and poured whiskey into the wound. Even being unconscious, Jeremy winced when the rotgut hit the open wound.

He pushed the bloody rags back and wound more rags around the leg and tied them off tight. "That's about all we can do for him right now. Keep that fire goin', Kleinfelt and we'll do what we can to keep this feller alive." He settled back into the dirt and motioned Kleinfelt to sit down.

"We're in a pickle, boy," he started.

"I wish you'd quit calling me boy, Pappy. I'm in my twenties, you know."

"You start acting like a man, I'll quit calling you boy. Now listen to me closely and don't give me no argument of any kind or I'm likely to shoot you. Those outlaws have kidnapped young Jeanne Moss and are probably riding high into that mountain range yonder. They've got most of the gold they stole from old Sherm Ahern's bank, and they're fixin' to do some bad things.

"When Jeremy wakes up, which won't be long now, I want you to take him back to Belmont and get him to the doc's. This is as important as anything you'll ever do in your life, so you listen to me. You find Marshal Tetford and tell him that I'm following the outlaws and you need to form a posse and come join me.

"With his own leg all shot up, Tetford ain't gonna be able ride with that posse. It's you that's got to bring them to me. You been wallowin' along like a little kid and don't want me to call you boy, well boy, here's your chance. Grow up.

"You bring that posse north to the Moss place and you'll see where I've rode off to, and you follow. I'll leave you plenty of sign. You don't want me to call you boy no more, you better be a man from this minute on. Little Jeanne Moss's life and mine will depend on you doing this right."

Pappy Somerset reached over and filled his hands with dirt, using it to wipe the blood away, stood up, and walked to his horse. "This is your chance to become a man," he said, mounted, and rode north toward the big ranch. He didn't turn and wave, didn't say another word, just rode off at a fast trot, leaving Kleinfelt sitting on the ground with a half-empty flask of whiskey to cleanse the wound one more time before he started the long ride to Belmont.

Timothy Kleinfelt had never overseen anything more than cleaning a horse stall before he pinned that little badge on, and now, he found himself sitting on the ground fully in charge of whether this man lying near him would die or not, whether that man's sister could be saved from an outlaw

45

gang, and whether he could raise a posse to come help Pappy Somerset.

He wanted to let the tears flow, just get on his horse and ride off. Run away. Cry out in shame. *I can't do this. It isn't fair. Why me?* The tears flowed down his red cheeks and he wrung his hands, kicked some dirt and heard Jeremy moan as he slowly woke up. Kleinfelt grabbed the canteen and as he let Jeremy sip some water knew he wanted to run away more than anything in the world.

"Thank you," Jeremy Moss whispered, coughing from drinking too fast.

Something clicked. Instead of running away, Tim Kleinfelt built up the fire and made a pot of coffee, pulled the bedroll off his saddle, spread it across young Jeremy, and took stock of what he had. *Basically, I'm more than a day out of Belmont, no food, little water, some whiskey, and saddlebags full of gold.* He had to snicker at his situation. *Just me and a wounded man and a sack full of gold!* He settled down into the dirt and laughed.

Yes sir, Mr. Somerset, it's time for me to grow up. He stood up, put more wood on the fire and took a short nip from the flask. "Not bad. Alright, Jeremy Moss, when you wake up all the way, I'm going to see to it that you live and then I'm going to help save your sister." It felt good to say it, but there was a nagging thought way in the back of his head that he might be telling one big lie.

Night came on fast high in the Monitor Range and the temperature plummeted along with daylight. The men sat around the fire eating roasted venison and drinking whiskey brought from the ranch. Jeanne Moss, bruised, and used terribly by all the men, was wrapped in a blanket, tied hand and foot, laid out near the fire, whimpering. She screamed, kicked, bit, scratched, and fought each man in turn, and was afraid that in the morning it would start all over again. She wanted to die. More than anything in the world, she wanted to die. The men smelled like an outhouse and were brutal in their treatment of her. Not one of them offered her a drink of water or a bite to eat.

All they wanted was to use her and get a moment's satisfaction. While they stood or sat close to the fire, she was shoved off to the side. Her wounds were bleeding and every muscle and bone was bruised. She could taste blood from where she had been hit in the mouth more than once, and she was having difficulty seeing out of her right eye from taking a fist thrown by Oliver.

Visions of her father's body spread across the ranch house entry, dead, mixed with the memory of what these horrible men did to her, and all Jeanne Moss wanted was to die. *No!* She thought all at once. *No, what I want is to see these men dead. So, help me, papa, I will see these men dead.*

Her eyes were looking off into the darkening forest planning how to get away. She knew Jeremy had tried to runaway but didn't know if he made it. Did those men shoot her brother too? She was raised on that ranch, chased cows in these mountains, heard her father say more than once that she wasn't afraid of anything.

I'm going to get myself untied and get away. I am. She worked hours trying but could not get the ropes loose. She rubbed them on rocks, to no avail, tried to stretch them and wasn't strong enough. But, Jeanne Moss did not give up.

She was sure they would use her and then discard her, dead. She tried to get free of her bonds, but couldn't. She was cold but couldn't break free. She cried, softly, until fear, cold, hunger, and pain faded into fitful sleep.

The outlaws drank until they passed out, one at a time. It was Humboldt Charley who dragged Jeanne off into the bushes one more time, before he too wrapped up in a blanket and passed out. Jeanne cried and whimpered until she too finally fell fast asleep, under some trees, far from the fire. She was kicked awake by George Oliver just as the sun made its presence known.

"Get up, girl," he snarled. He grabbed her arm, spun her around and untied her hands. He was about to lead her deeper into the trees for another round of terror.

"Leave her be," Humboldt Charley snarled from the fire. "You've had your share, Oliver."

"She's beggin' for more, Charley," Oliver laughed, continuing to drag her and the blanket across the rocks and dirt.

"Leave her be, I said." Charley stood up, a coffee cup in his left hand, a forty-five in his right. He stood with his legs slightly spread and Oliver heard the hammer being pulled fully back and knew it would take just a twitch to let it fall back. "Set her down and have some coffee."

Oliver looked at Charley, looked down at the girl and remembered just how fine it had been the day before. *So young and sweet.* George Oliver let go of the girl and turned to walk back to the fire, and Charley slowly eased the hammer down and started to put the gun back in the holster.

Oliver grabbed for his gun, spinning off to the side and died as two forty-five bullets tore into him, one from Humboldt Charley's weapon, and one from Enos Payson's. Payson had anticipated what that fool Oliver might try, and had been standing a few feet from Charley. Jeanne screamed when she saw Oliver's body flung back from the impact. Blood was pumping from the two wounds, splashing onto the girl.

Charley and Payson joined Buford Gamble for another cup of coffee, packed their horses, and rode out of camp. It was at least an hour later that Jeanne woke up and found herself alone, high in the mountains, looking into the dead eyes of George Oliver. The flies had found him, too, and she crawled away as fast as she could. All she had on was the ripped and torn nightgown. She didn't know when she lost the robe, and discovered they even took her blanket when they left.

Tears overflowed, ran down her filthy cheeks and she sat down on a rock near the still smoldering fire. Jeanne was a tough little ranch girl, but she'd been abused, bruised, and frightened more than she had ever been in her life. "I can't just sit here and feel sorry for myself," she muttered after about half an hour's good cry. She stirred the fire, found wood to get it going good, and knew she had to have something to wear when night came.

I was sure they were going to kill me, and I guess, leaving me alone in these mountains, they believe they have. Well, you miserable men, you haven't killed me. I've ridden in these mountains all my life. She was determined that she would find her way down out of the hills and back to her home.

I've got to protect myself, it'll be cold tonight, and I must get off this mountain. She also knew she had to fight off the fear, the terror of what might be close by. A bear? A lion? Another man or men? *I need clothes, boots, food, and a gun, and right now, I ain't got any of those things.*

She searched for her robe and couldn't find it, couldn't find anything, despite hoping the outlaws had forgotten something. "What would Pa do?" She whispered out loud and sat back down on the rock. She caught herself looking at Oliver's dead body. "I can't do that, Pa," she murmured, as if he had made the suggestion. Two hours later, Jeanne Moss was dressed in pants, shirt, boots, and jacket, a couple sizes too large.

She also had a forty-five caliber Colt in a fine leather holster and belt. She was sitting on a rock thanking about big Bill Moss and what he used to say about this country. "Go downhill," she said, and stood up, slipped the belted weapon over her head and around her neck so it hung to the side, and followed the hoof prints the outlaws had made coming up, back downhill.

"I'm as good a shot as Pa was, and I know how to start a fire with just wood sticks. The first thing I see that looks edible, I'm gonna shoot." There was determination in the girl, but also a touch of fear and anxiety, and lingering pain from her ordeal.

Jeanne Moss remembered crossing many streams on the ride up and knew she would not die of thirst. She knew how to start a fire the hard way, without a striker or kerosene, and knew how to shoot. *Those foul men even took the rest of that venison with them. I swear, Pa, when I can, I will track those men down and kill them. I swear to you.*

Pappy Somerset rode slowly up to the ranch house and stepped off his tired horse. "They didn't even bother to bury old Bill," he muttered, walking onto the veranda porch. He made a fast search of the house and came back out to bury Bill Moss. "I'm gonna be killing me some real bastards when I find them," he said several times before mounting his horse and hitting the trail.

He followed the five horses easily north on the main road and saw where they took a trail east, along a stream. He knew the country well, had hunted the country often, for deer, antelope, and elk. The outlaws weren't trying very hard to hide their trail and Pappy made good time, but knew he would run out of daylight well before finding the gang.

It was late in the afternoon when he spotted a cottontail near the creek and popped it. "This'll be better'n that jack last night," he chuckled, cleaning and skinning the fat little rabbit. He made up a camp back away from the stream, watered his horse and tied him off.

"I've spent most of my life sitting in little camps like this," he muttered. "A nice fire, good supper, and fair skies. 'Course back when I was with the army, we were far north in the

Rockies and the Black Hills, and we got hit by some blizzards that I knew would be the death of me. Hell, a man's piss would freeze before it hit the ground," and he had to chuckle at the thought.

"It's been thirty years since I tracked something that would kill me if it got the chance and that I will kill when I get the chance. Feels good, it does. I'm worried about the young deputy. I'm gonna need some heavy backup and if that boy folds his hand, I could be the dead one. Don't know who raised that boy but they sure didn't turn him into a man."

Morning found him on the trail before the sun was fully up. "They were moving fast yesterday," he muttered as he followed their trail. "Don't seem to care that I might just be coming along behind them." He stopped at mid-day for a short breather. The trail he was following was steep, meandering through deep forest and then into rocks and canyons.

"That one horse with the busted shoe is gonna come lame if they don't do something about that, and I surely hope they don't," he said. He left marks on rocks, laid out sticks and rocks along the way for Kleinfelt and his posse to see when they came. "They won't even be leaving Belmont until sometime tomorrow, I reckon. Hopefully I'll have these fools pinned down by then."

Like most of the old men who spent their time alone in the wilds, Pappy Somerset talked to himself, to the trees and rocks, and always to his horse or mule. Often complete conversations would take place and decisions were made. "I'm gonna catch up with those boys tomorrow," he said.

There was no doubt in Pappy Somerset's mind that he would catch and hold the bank robbing gang. It was just a matter of time. Thinking about Smithson getting shot at the bank, about Marshal Tetford getting shot during the chase, and Bill Moss being killed right at his own front door was more than enough to keep Pappy's anger up and his desire to catch the men.

Add to that, they had abducted young Jeanne Moss, and Pappy's anger soared. "That poor, dear girl," he said. The thought of what she must be going through brought rage and tears to the old scout, and he urged his tired horse a little faster. The country was rough, and the gang had a good head start on him, but at least the trail wasn't that hard to follow.

"They don't really care whether or not they're being followed." He remembered one time, many years past, when he was tracking a band of Sioux warriors who had attacked a small outpost near the Black Hills and abducted a young girl. *It took us five days to catch up with them varmints and that girl suffered each and every one of those days. I'll catch up tomorrow, Jeanne. I promise I will.*

CHAPTER 6

KLEINFELT HAD A MISERABLE RIDE BACK TO BELMONT, TRYING to stem the flow of blood from Jeremy's wound, trying to keep the boy in the saddle and awake, and knowing he had to get back as quickly as possible. He ran out of daylight while they were still well out from Belmont, and he made a small camp with a good fire. *No food for hungry Tim tonight*, he wanted to whimper and caught himself. *And none of that self-pity, either.*

Reflection of any kind is rare in young people and intro-spection is even more rare, but some of the things Pappy Somerset had said to and about Kleinfelt worked their way into his young mind. It was the constant reference to him being a boy that penetrated deep, and the first response had been denial, then questions, and finally, acceptance. The young man had become aware of his shortcomings.

He spent long hours walking the two horses and carrying on a conversation with himself and the horses. Jeremy Moss was unconscious most of the time. "Other than Pappy, the only other adult who has ever tried to talk to me or teach me something is Marshal Tetford. I didn't pay any more atten-tion to what he was saying than I did to Pappy. I don't mind sayin' it, since ain't no one to hear me, I'm scared. What if Jeremy dies? Will they blame me?"

Alone, since Jeremy spent more time unconscious than alert, in a saddle in the middle of the vast Monitor Valley of central Nevada gave Kleinfelt all the time and space needed for deep self-reflection, and in those long hours the boy reached out for maturity.

He had a good fire going, had Jeremy wrapped in a blanket, and knew he had to change the dressing on that wound. It was bad enough the night before having to clean and skin that rabbit, how would he clean that wound? He found an old shirt in a saddlebag and ripped it into pieces to make a bandage, got the flask of whiskey out, and started work.

"Ouch," Jeremy howled. "That really hurts."

Kleinfelt jumped back. "I didn't realize you were awake, Jeremy. Sorry, but I've got to get this wound cleaned up. Looks like some infection has started to set in. Hang on, I'll try to be as careful as I can."

"Is that you, deputy? Where's Pappy Somerset? Where are we?"

"We're about fifteen miles out from Belmont. We'll have you at the doc's as quick as possible tomorrow. Do you remember what happened at the ranch?"

"Four men rode in, shot pa, shot me, and I got the chance to run and did. They have Jeanne. Where's Pappy?"

"He's chasing those outlaws, Jeremy. After I get you to Belmont, I'm forming a posse and will ride back to help Pappy. They robbed the bank in Belmont, killed old Mr. Smithson and Marshal Tetford got shot chasing them."

The two slept on empty stomachs and started their ride into town just as the sun peaked over the high ridges of the Monitor Range. It was a long ride with several stops as Jeremy Moss had lost so much blood and was almost too weak to keep himself in the saddle. They were able to find water, but had to stop once to rebuild the bandage as it slipped and heavy bleeding started again.

Kleinfelt and Moss rode straight to the doctor's home-office and the deputy helped get Jeremy off his horse. Doc Patterson came running out to help get Jeremy inside. "Shot in the leg, doc. Just like the marshal. Where's the marshal, do you know?" Kleinfelt was talking fast and knew it had taken a long time to get back to town.

"He's in the back, Tim. He can't get out of bed yet. That leg is badly broke, and he might not ever walk right again." Doc Patterson kept four or five beds in two rooms at the back of his home as a hospital. "You'll find him in number one."

Old Doc like to say that. Each of his beds had letters associated with them, and each of the two rooms had its own number. He worked in the hospital in Sacramento years ago and liked the concept of organization. "Should find him in Bed A, room Number One," he said again, with a smile. "All right, Jeremy, let's see what kind of trouble you've gotten into."

Morning splashed its colorful arrival across the peaks of the mountains and found Terrence Corcoran tending a small fire, boiling a pot of coffee, and frying a pan full of trout he'd caught the day before. "One or two more days and I'll have had my fair share of the idle life," he said, pouring a cup of coffee. "All my bruises and bumps are about healed; my mind is once again as sharp as a chunk of firewood." He chuckled at his idea of a joke, "and I'll have to give some thought to finding a job somewhere." He put aside talk for a minute, swilling some coffee and turning the trout.

Corcoran was a man who lived free, carried a badge more often than not, made his living with a gun, a strong body, and a quick mind, and he had to laugh at where he was and what he was doing. "Idling away another day in the high mountains. I might have been in the fur business if I'd been alive during those times. I've been offered good positions with the army in their quest to annihilate the Indians. But, the fact is, I don't believe in what they're doing."

Again, he laughed out loud. "I'm sitting here with busted ribs, bruises, and gashes all over my body from an encounter with some damn fool wild Indians and I just said I don't believe in the government's passion to rid the country of Indians. I've fought 'em, lived with 'em, even loved a few of prettier ones, but damn it all, they were here first."

Fried potatoes and hot coffee went down with the fresh trout, he thought about cold sage grouse for lunch in a few hours, and gave serious thought to a nap. "No," he murmured, "I need to give serious thought to what I'm going to be doing when I leave this mountain.

"Fred Seagram offered me that deputy's badge in Eureka and I might just take him up on that. I love that country around there, and there are some mighty pretty young ladies living out on those ranches that will need my protectin'." He nursed his breakfast into an hour-long talk with himself and decided that maybe it would be a good time to take a walk and see if he could scare up another sage hen.

"You just stay here and eat grass, Rube. I'll be back in a couple of hours." He gave the horse a good rubdown, found his fowling piece and some rounds, and walked off across a broad, flat, rock infested ridge. The broad rim dropped off into a forest-filled canyon. The creek that splashed across the plateau near his camp flung itself over the rimrock and was flowing through the forest and into a canyon.

On the flat ridge, the sagebrush was thick and there were a few scattered stands of brushy cedar and piñon pine. "I dub thee Flat Top Ridge," he chuckled, wending his way through the brush. It was as if the mountainside had been shaved and flattened. All the surrounding hillsides were nicely rounded off, filled with heavy timber, but not this one.

He came to the western most edge of the ridge and two big sage hens lifted off, giving him a start. He watched them fly, low and slow, but didn't raise his weapon. "Too early," he muttered. "If I shot you, I'd have to go back to camp." He made his way off the ridge and down into a heavy stand of timber. Big pines and spruce, some aspen, big red cedar, and cottonwood.

"Whoa," he said, stopping quickly, holding his nose. The stench of death was more than strong. "Something big died around here, close." He quit thinking about good tasting birds and started thinking like the lawman he was. He followed his nose down through the trees and onto a small flat area with a fire ring still warm.

"This is interesting," he said. "Something big and dead close by and a camp fire with warm embers. I'm thinkin' something bad happened around here." He stood still and listened for any kind of movement or crying, looked all around the little flat areas and saw nothing.

Corcoran laid the shotgun up against a big rock, opened his jacket and checked his sidearm for loads. It didn't take long to find George Oliver's body, naked and bloated, covered in flies. "Somebody didn't much care for this guy. Shot him twice and stole his clothes."

He walked back to the fire and saw tiny footprints made by someone barefoot. "This is strange. No boots or shoes, but those prints don't go anywhere." He wandered around the area and found where horses had been tethered. "Horse prints go off northeast and one set of boot prints go off southwest. And somebody, small, maybe a girl? Wandering around without boots. I wonder what happened here?"

Corcoran spent more time checking out the prints that were in and around the camp area, found Jeanne's nightgown, ripped and bloody. "Something bad happened here." He picked up his shotgun and made tracks back to his camp, saddled Rube, made sure his rifle was fully loaded, and rode back to where Oliver's body was rotting. He couldn't get the idea of a girl in a nightgown and no boots being in that camp, and the nightgown, bloody and ripped, taken from her.

"We are miles from nowhere, high in the mountains. I can't imagine what I've stumbled on, can't imagine what happened or why, for that matter." He spent some time going over the little campsite once more.

Jeanne was having a hard time walking the trail down off the high mountain in oversize boots. Besides all the pain from being severely beaten, and horribly abused, the boots were raising welts and blisters that made her cry out often. She slipped as a rock turned under her boot and fell head-long into more rocks, banging her head as she went down.

She had been on the trail about an hour, was hungry and sore, and now was sitting under a large rock, facing away from the trail, nursing a bloody head. She couldn't help it; she burst into tears, crying as she had never cried before, calling for her pa, calling for Jeremy, almost wailing her sorrow.

So much terror for a sixteen-year-old girl, so much pain, thirst, hunger, and worst of all, humiliation. Through her crying and moaning it came to her that all of this had taken place within one day's time.

The reality of her situation began to set in, shoving aside the remembered terror and replacing it with a new terror. Through her tears, she was mumbling. "I've never been this alone. I'm hurt, hungry, and thirsty, and I don't know how far from the ranch we rode yesterday." She was tucked in under a rock on a cold autumn day with no fire.

"I'm not going to die out here. I'm not!" The clothes she

took from Oliver were filthy, but she used the hem of the shirt to wipe the blood from her head. She could feel the knot growing from where she bounced off the rocks, and got the bleeding mostly under control. She couldn't stop the tears, though, and when she tried to get up, discovered she had twisted her ankle when the rock turned.

Jeanne cried out in pain and plopped back down. She pulled the boot off and found her ankle swelling up and sore to the touch. "God, I'll never get that boot back on, never be able to get wood to start a fire, and never be able to kill something for food." The sobbing increased, and she beat the ground with the boot, her anger taking control. "I'm not a little baby and I'm not gonna die out here." She almost snarled it out through her tears and slammed the boot into the ground again. "I'm not."

Bill Moss would tell anyone who would listen that Jeanne was far tougher than Jeremy could ever hope to be, was a fine horseman, could ride anything with four feet, and could out rope him. "She's one tough little filly, boys, let me tell you. Whatever man she sets her sights on better be the toughest hombre around." Jeanne could almost hear him saying this as she quelled the tears and made ready to get back on the trail.

The tears and toughness ebbed when she found she really couldn't get the boot back on over her swollen ankle. She had Oliver's gun belt and pistol and mumbled, "That stupid man didn't carry a knife."

Corcoran found the boot prints leading out of the camp area most intriguing and followed them down a trail. "Whoever made these prints doesn't seem to have much sense of direction," he mused. "Or is going the opposite direction the horses took for a reason?" He wanted to chuckle thinking about it, but also understood that whoever walked in the opposite direction was hurt or in some other kind of trouble.

It wasn't a difficult decision to follow the boot prints.

"Seems that one person was left behind and very dead, and another alive, and the alive one might have been the owner of that bloody nightgown, which might be why the dead man is naked. Whoever made the boot prints is probably in deep trouble about now."

He got off his horse after an hour or so to look closely at what he was following. "I see, now," he muttered. "There's a group of horses going up the trail and one person walking down the trail, following it back down. I wonder what the hell happened at that campsite?"

Another hour of slow tracking and Corcoran stopped to give him and his horse a breather. He stepped down and walked to a small stand of grass to let Rube graze, pulled his canteen down and took a long pull of chilled water. That's when he heard whimpering. He stepped away from Rube, so he could hear better and thought the sounds were like a child's crying.

He walked around a large rock fall and almost stumbled into Jeanne Moss sitting in a rock pile, whimpering on the one hand but with anger flushing her face on the other. She had a bloody head and was holding an oversize boot. Corcoran didn't want to frighten the girl any more than she obviously already was. "Miss," he said, quietly, "are you hurt?"

Jeanne jumped, startled, and cowered, her back plastered against the rocks. "No," she whispered. "No. Stay away. No. I'll scream," she cried. *Oh, God, they're back. I'll kill the first man that tries to touch me. I will.*

He saw bruises on her face, blood in her hair and a good-sized lump, too. He saw rage, fear, and desperation in those large eyes. He wanted to chuckle seeing this little girl, just a teenager he figured, dressed in a big man's clothing. *I don't know who might have done this, but that person is now in my sights. What kind of animal would do this?* He noticed her ankle was swollen to almost twice what it should be.

"I'm not here to hurt you, miss. My name's Corcoran, Terrence Corcoran, and I stumbled onto the camp you left. I'm here to help." *There were four men and a girl in that camp, and now one man is dead, one little girl has been horribly attacked, and three men will have to face me very soon.*

The say the Irish are born poets and Corcoran had been known to sally forth with the lyrics of the gods, but this Irishman worshiped at the feet of the ladies and would not tolerate one being abused in any way. *I'll not allow myself to leave this earth until I have found the men responsible for this. Despicable vermin did this and they'll meet me and know they are in hell.*

She wouldn't look at him, cowered and drew her knees up tight, wrapped her arms around her legs, tucked her head into her knees, and sobbed, "No. No!" She knew the weapon was sitting just a few feet away and was about to reach for when the big man stepped back away from her.

"I'm not going to hurt you, miss," he said gently. Corcoran gathered some wood and got a little fire going, brought Rube over near, got the canteen and put it next to the girl, telling her it was there.

He saw the gun belt and pistol in its leather and picked it up. "This must have come along with the clothing," he muttered. He checked it and found it fully loaded, and slung the belt over his shoulder.

He stepped back to Rube, fussed through his saddlebags and found some smoked venison, some pemmican, and a dried-up biscuit. "Ah, here we go," he chuckled, coming up with a tin of coffee and a small flask of brandy. "Just what the doctor ordered."

Jeanne reached out for the canteen and drank deep of the chilled spring water and watched the tall, strong man build the fire, make coffee, and bring her a cup. "You're kinda young, but would you like a taste of brandy in that coffee? It might make you feel a little bit better. Then we can talk. Again, miss, I'm not here to hurt you. You've been hurt more than anyone should ever be hurt. We'll get this all figured out." He smiled, and she responded with the slightest of smiles.

It must be his eyes. I've seen big strong men with good smiles, but their eyes deceive them. His are soft and honest. Can I really trust him, or did he come back from the others? No, Pa would tell me to be wary and wait for the trust to build. It's building.

"What's your name?"

"Jeanne," she said. "Jeanne Moss. Those men killed my pa and shot my brother," and she started crying again, thinking about the terrible things they had done to her. The whimpering was more than Corcoran could handle.

"Please, don't cry, Jeanne. Was that your brother I found at that camp?

Her eyes flared wide open and said, "No! He's a horrible man. A brute. All of them were, but he was the worst."

"I've got a small camp up on Flat Top Ridge, with food and blankets. Let's go up there, I'll tend to your wounds and get you fed and warm, and then we'll ride for help. I'm not one right now, but I've worked as a deputy sheriff and I promise I won't hurt you at all."

She didn't want him to touch her, glared in anger when he made a move to help her up, but softened some, when she looked up into his brilliant green eyes, saw his long reddish hair hanging in curls and waves, and nodded. "You need to kill those men," she whispered, her eyes blazing with hatred. "They are monsters and you need to kill them."

"We'll get you safe and warm, and then I'll work on that little problem," he said.

With hot coffee and a splash of brandy mixed in, and with some pemmican, old and chewy, Jeanne felt strong enough to ride behind Corcoran. He bandaged her head and wrapped her ankle, lifted her onto the horse behind him, and they made the long ride back to his camp. He skirted her old camp, not wanting to bring back all those memories.

Whatever happened back there must have been horrible. I was thinking about finding a new job, I think I just found one. Get her safe and kill whoever did this to her.

CHAPTER 7

"THIS ISN'T AS EASY A TRAIL AS I THOUGHT," PAPPY SOMERSET murmured, moving his horse through heavy timber, up steep hills, and around large rock formations. There were towering peaks and deep canyons, broad plains and massive palisades to move through or around. "I can't tell if these jaspers know where they're goin', or just following the terrain." He wasn't having any trouble reading their trail. He was following it as it wandered about. "Just how high in this range of mountains are these fools planning to go?"

From time to time he could look across the wide Monitor Valley to the double peaked Mount Jefferson in the Toquima Range, knowing those peaks were over eleven thousand feet. He figured he was already close to eight thousand feet and the Monitors topped out at over ten thousand. "If they do go all the across the top, they could turn north toward Eureka."

He couldn't keep his mind off Jeanne Moss and the troubles he knew she was facing. "Just sixteen," he said over and over. "She must know her father's dead, that she will just be a toy to these bastards until they tire of her. I have to get to her before that."

He'd filled his saddlebags with food from the Moss ranch

before leaving, had two canteens of water but knew there were streams all along the length of the mountains. He added a couple of blankets from Moss's, and was trailing a saddled horse in anticipation of saving Jeanne. "Been doing this most of my life," he muttered late that day, setting up a quick camp alongside a stream gaily splashing its way off the mountain.

Being there any other time, under any other circumstances, and Pappy would have had a broad smile on his face as he arranged camp. The sky was clear and as he had made his way higher into the craggy mountains, the air was cooler and incredibly fragrant. It was late summer in the valley and early fall in the high country, but the only thing on Pappy's mind was saving Jeanne Moss and killing outlaws.

The Monitor Range was home to black bears, wolves, mountain lions and coyotes, and Pappy had his grub wrapped in canvas and hanging from a lower limb on a pine tree and slept well away from that tree. He remembered one-time, back in the 1860s, somewhere in New Mexico country, a black bear climbed the tree, and then pulled the grub sack up to him, ripped it open, ate all the bacon, and left the rest.

The coyote is more cunning, but nothing beats a black bear for smarts when it smells bacon or smoked buffalo. They'll follow their nose five hunnert miles for either one.

A quick supper, good sleep, and early rising found Pappy tired and stiff, pouring that first cup of coffee as the sky woke up with intense colors and chilly temperatures. "Looks like a good day, anyway," he said, saddling the horses for another long ride. It was almost mid-day when the trail got jumbled up a bit.

"What have we got here?" he said. "All the horses going up this trail, but now, we have someone walking down the trail, and another horse, not a part of the outlaw gang, going down. There," he pointed. "That new horse going up again. Looks like an intersection in Denver," he chuckled.

Pappy Somerset loved reading trail sign, and wished there had been a young lieutenant standing next to him, so he could show the kid what he was seeing. "Some learned, some scoffed. Some lived, some died," he chortled, tying off the horses and looking closely at the signs in the dirt.

It didn't take him ten minutes to find where Corcoran had built a fire and made coffee around behind that rock fall. He found a bloody bandage and indications of two people, one wearing only one boot, and the barefoot print was very small. "Jeanne Moss," he almost whispered. "This other rider has her. Well, you won't have her for long, buster," Pappy said, mounting and starting up Corcoran's trail.

Terrence Corcoran eased the girl down from Rube and stepped off, tying the horse off. Riding across Flat Top Ridge they kicked up two sage hens and Corcoran thought about the one he had let live earlier that morning. "We'll have to satisfy ourselves with some smoked venison for supper, Jeanne," he chuckled.

After getting her settled and wrapped in a blanket in front of a welcome fire, he asked, "What exactly brought all this on, Jeanne? Who were those men who abducted you?"

She looked at this long tall man who had the most wonderful smile and felt safe for the first time in two days. "I don't know," she whimpered. "It was early morning and I heard horses riding in, heard Pa open the front door and say something, and then two gunshots. I ran downstairs and saw Jeremy running toward the house and one of the men shot him." She closed her eyes, tried to hold back the tears, but couldn't.

He wanted to gather her up in his arms and hug. He also knew that after what she had gone through it would be one of the worst things he could do. *She won't want a man's arms wrapped around those shoulders for a long time.* He had gained her trust, and this wasn't the time to lose it.

"Where is your ranch?" Corcoran asked. "It's too late to start out today, so first thing tomorrow we'll start back down off this mountain and get you home."

"We're toward the north end of the Monitor Valley, about thirty miles or so north of Belmont. All our hands are up on summer range gathering for the drive down."

"Did those men say where they might be going?" *Something must have happened before to make those men simply ride onto the ranch and shoot her pa. Did they take her for their pleasure or for insurance? Is there a posse somewhere down that mountain?*

"Was any particular one of them outstanding in any way? Dress, accent, behavior? Did they talk about anything?" Corcoran didn't want to press too hard, which might cause her to shut down.

"Yeah," she said, tilting her head to one side, remembering. "One was really mean and wore a feather, an eagle feather I think, in his hat. He had mean little pig-eyes, and all the men seemed afraid of him." She shivered just thinking about what had happened with that man. "He was the worst."

"Humboldt Charley," Corcoran muttered, slapping a piece of wood onto the fire.

"They called him Charley, yes." Jeanne Moss shivered again, remembering how mean, ugly, and always angry Charley had been. "He shot the man you found, and these are that man's clothes. Charley was really angry when my brother was able to escape. There were saddle bags on the horse Jeremy took that were full of gold, he said."

She watched him in fascination almost seeing his mind work after she answered each of his questions. With each question, with each of his gestures, each time he added wood to the fire, she felt a little safer. *Pa always said the Irishmen were just romantic fools filled with poetry and gibberish. I like Terrence Corcoran's gibberish.*

"They must have been running from a robbery of some kind. The nearest place to your ranch would be Belmont, right Jeanne?" She nodded and poured the two of them some fresh coffee. "Heading into the mountains like this, they must be planning on working down the other side and toward Eureka.

"That would be a fair ride right now, but if an early storm came through, they probably wouldn't make it."

"Then I'm praying for a monster blizzard to come right now," she said, and when he laughed, she did too. "I mean it, I'm going to pray for a blizzard to kill those men. If they don't kill them, you have to, Corcoran."

Corcoran gathered more wood for the fire, had more coffee boiling, and was about to warm some smoked venison for their supper when he heard hooves scraping on rocks. He motioned for Jeanne to stay still and quiet, pulled his heavy Colt and moved slowly through the brush toward the sound.

She cowered in the blanket, had her knees drawn up tight, eyes mashed shut, fearing the outlaws had returned. *No. No, it can't be them. Even wild Indians would be better. Kill whoever it is, Corcoran.*

Corcoran saw a man leading two horses, slowly, concentrating on the trail he was following. The man carried a rifle and stopped suddenly, lifting his head. *He smells coffee and our fire,* Corcoran almost chuckled, and in a strong but not menacing voice said, "Hold it right there, Pard."

Pappy Somerset froze, looked around and spotted Corcoran standing near some high sage, a Colt Peacemaker leveled at him. "Who are you and what do you want?" Corcoran asked quietly. "Don't mess with me cuz I'm already some riled."

"Name's Somerset. Chasing some bank robbers what abducted a young girl. I think you might be holding her. Got a posse comin' up behind me, so you'd be wise to turn her over." Pappy Somerset was looking down the barrel of that revolver but was talking as if he had the drop on Corcoran. He saw a tall man with death in his eyes and way about him that said he didn't lose these kinds of encounters. Well, Pappy didn't either and one of them might die at any moment.

"Ease the rifle back in its leather, Mr. Somerset and come on in. Name's Corcoran, Terrence Corcoran and you'll find Miss Jeanne Moss sitting by the fire having a cup of coffee. We need to talk, sir."

As soon as Jeanne saw Pappy she jumped up and hobbled toward him, her ankle not willing to cooperate. "Pappy," she wailed, throwing herself at him. Pappy Somerset was an old timer in the Monitor Valley, and a friend to every ranch kid the length of the valley. He remembered all their birthdays, taught many of them the pleasures of fishing, and had fun teaching them how to get along in the great outdoors. He liked to say he had an entire valley full of trackers-in-training.

He helped her back to her blankets and squatted down next to her. He had to chuckle seeing her dressed in filthy men's clothing miles too big for her. Corcoran added some wood to the fire, poured himself and Pappy Somerset some coffee, and sat down.

"Glad you're here with that extra horse, Somerset. We're planning to ride off the mountain in the morning and it would have been a difficult ride. Tell me about this bank robbing gang and how you're involved."

"I will," Pappy said, "and then you can tell me how you became involved." The conversation lasted well past sunset and late into the night. Corcoran was twenty-five years or more, younger than Somerset but they had been in many of the same places, knew many of the same people, and had little respect for young army officers who rarely accepted advice from their elders.

Corcoran stirred the sunrise fire and got the coffee boiling fast. Pappy tended to Jeanne's wounds and watched the sun explode across the sky. "I love mornings," he said. "It smells good, it feels good, and makes me want to do something."

Jeanne had to chuckle, listening to him carry on. Her pa had taught her to fish, but it was Pappy taught her how to start a fire with flint and steel, how to follow a wounded deer, and how to shoot a rabbit with a rifle and not ruin an ounce of meat.

Corcoran handed him a mug of coffee. "Yup," is all he said, turning to tend some side meat he had frying."

"So, Terrence Corcoran, what's your plan?"

"Get this girl back home safe and jump on this gang's trail. Ain't gonna let them get away with what they did to that poor darlin'. Ain't no man alive got that right, and every one of them is gonna pay the price."

Jeanne was listening from inside her blankets and thought that she would want to be standing next to this wild Irishman when he did put the bunch into the ground.

"Want company?" is all Pappy Somerset said, a gentle smile spread across his ancient face. "Bill Moss could be a bastard when he wanted to, but no little girl should ever have to face what Jeanne did."

"Yup," is all Corcoran said and a partnership was formed. It took them two days to get back down off the mountain and to Moss's ranch. Jeanne's ankle wasn't broken but was twisted and she was in pain most of the ride. She said more than once that all she wanted was her own boots and clothes to wear.

"We can't just ride off and leave her here, alone,"

Corcoran said. "When will the cow hands be down with the herds?"

"Not for some time, Terrence," she said. "I'll be fine. For several years it's just been me, Jeremy, and pa, so I can take care of things until the men get back."

The point became moot the next morning when Timothy Kleinfelt led four men onto the ranch. Pappy Somerset saw a different Tim Kleinfelt immediately and whacked the young man across the shoulders. "Glad you're here, deputy. Everybody alive back in Belmont?"

"Marshal Tetford and Jeremy have casts on their legs and spend a lot of time complaining."

"Good," Pappy chuckled. "Meet Terrence Corcoran. He saved Jeanne and has an idea of where those fools might be heading. We're going after 'em."

"Mr. Corcoran. I'm Tim Kleinfelt, deputy marshal in Belmont. Marshal Tetford said he's sure the gang is the Humboldt Charley gang, by the descriptions the banker gave him."

"I know those bastards," Corcoran said, "and when Jeanne described that one man, it had to be Humboldt Charley They've stole cattle and robbed banks from Salt Lake to Reno. I was on my way to Eureka to go to work for Sheriff Fred Seagram when all this took place. The trail those men took would take them right toward Eureka, so I think Pappy and I will light out right away."

"Don't even think about coming with us, Tim," Pappy said. "With Tetford laid up, your first responsibility is to the citizens of Belmont. You've come a long way in a short time, Deputy Kleinfelt. Keep it up."

They had supplies from the Moss ranch on Corcoran's mule and the two men rode out north, heading for the road that led from Austin to Eureka, hoping to get there in two days at best, probably three. "Kleinfelt was a lot like Fetterman, back at Powder River, Corcoran." Pappy sounded like he had a story to tell. "Had his own thoughts and they were wrong most of the time. The difference being, Kleinfelt had time to learn and Fetterman wouldn't take that time.

"Sounded like you know a lot about this Humboldt Charley. Had dealings with him?"

"Twice, Pappy. Once up in Elko County and once way up north near a place called Goose Lake. Pitt River Indians were raisin' hell in that area, stealing cattle, threatening ranchers, and most of the activity turned out to be Humboldt Charley, not the tribe itself. Never have even seen the man," Corcoran laughed. "But when I do, he's a dead man. No man has the right to do what he did to Jeanne Moss."

"It's an ugly world, Mr. Corcoran. An ugly world, indeed."

"I like to think I can make it a little more attractive, Mr. Somerset. Yes sir, I do."

At the first night's camp, Pappy asked, "You ever serve?"

"No, Pappy, and never felt much like I wanted to. I was too young for that war between the states and more often than not I find myself on the side of the Indians in their fights with the army. We ain't treatin' them people right and I'd rather not be on what I consider the wrong side."

"I don't have a lot of Sioux friends, being an army scout and all, but I do have Crow and Shoshone friends. Met some Nez Percé that I found to be charming. The Sioux and the rest of the tribes are gonna lose this war simply because of the overwhelming numbers of white soldiers and immigrants flooding the plains and the west."

The fire was just embers when they finished more than one pot of coffee, drained a flask, and rolled into their blankets, watching a sky full of billions of stars brighten the night. "Ever wonder how far those little specks of light are from here?" Corcoran pointed toward the heavens. "Ever wonder just what they are?" His only answer was a bit of a harrumph, which made him smile.

"In a way, Pappy, I feel sorry for old Charley when the two of us catch up with him." He got a quiet little chuckle back and let his eyes slowly close.

"That's the sheriff's office over there," Corcoran said, leading his mule and Pappy Somerset up to a hitching rail. "And that big ugly brute walking out the door is Sheriff Fred Seagram." He waved stepping off Dude. "Mornin' Fred. You limpin', old man?"

"Wish you'd been here yesterday, Corcoran. Got shot, damn it. Who's that with you?" Seagram helped tie off the mule and ushered the group into the office. He eased down into a cane back chair, letting one leg stand out straight and Corcoran could see blood through his pant leg.

"Fred Seagram meet Pappy Somerset. We're following Humboldt Charley. He robbed the bank in Belmont, killed a rancher and kidnapped the rancher's daughter. Think he's headed this way. Who shot you?"

"You're late, Corcoran," Seagram snapped. "Humboldt Charley hit the bank here yesterday, killed old Elmer Shanks. I've got Deputy Foster and two men on their trail. There's nobody else available in town. Looks to be going north, probably toward the marshes." He shook his head, let his hand run across the wounded leg, and admitted, "Humboldt Charley shot me.

"Pappy Somerset, eh? I've heard your name when I worked up in the Black Hills. Nice to meet you." They shook hands and Seagram took a cup of coffee offered by Corcoran. "Got some sweetener for that," Seagram said. He opened a desk drawer and passed a flask around.

"They hit the Belmont bank just after the army paid off the ranchers for their stock and remounts. Something like that here?" Corcoran asked.

"Looks like it. Wells Fargo dropped off a shipment from the Carson City mint a few days ago. Don't know how they would have known about that, though, being over in the Monitor Valley. Maybe just dumb luck. You working for Tetford?"

"Nope, I came to claim my deputy badge from you, Fred," Corcoran laughed. "I just stumbled into all this, but it's gotten mighty personal. Swear me in, Fred, and send me out to catch or kill that bastard."

No woman who found herself in trouble would ever find a better friend or defender than Terrence Corcoran. From soiled doves working in horrible conditions to charming ladies in silks and furs to young girls kidnapped and abused by bank robbers, Corcoran would be their shining knight. "If you could have seen what those men did to that charming little girl and heard her tale, Fred, …" Corcoran choked up and took that opportunity to sip his coffee.

"Sounds to me like you got your Irish up 'bout as high as I've seen. You got your little bumps and bruises healed up? I did promise you that badge," Seagram chuckled.

Seagram reached into a desk drawer and found a beat up, bent and twisted, star badge and handed it to Corcoran. "Go get 'em, Irish, and be just as mean as you want to be. You want a badge, Pappy Somerset?"

"Not my place to refuse an order from you, Sheriff," he smiled, extending an open palm. Seagram laughed and put an equally used tin badge in the old man's hand.

"Star Café's open, Terrence. You boys get something to eat, sign the ticket, and hurry back with good news."

"I hope young Carmelita is still working there," Corcoran said. He and Pappy put up their horses and the mule, found a room at the hotel, and headed for the Star Café. "She's a charming lass, Pappy. Makes some fine enchiladas, and makes apple pie to make your mouth water thinkin' about."

"Terrence," Carmelita howled, racing across the small diner and flinging herself into his arms. "I thought you had left me. Didn't even say goodbye," she smiled and whimpered at the same time.

"I couldn't leave you, Carmelita. You'll always be with me, here," and he patted his heart. "Think you could feed a couple of hungry old lawdogs?"

"For you, only the best. Who is this with you, Terrence Corcoran?"

"Carmelita, meet Pappy Somerset, and be careful, he's been known to steel hearts."

She gave Pappy a warm hug and the two big men sat down to a full-fledged Mexican feast that lasted into the night.

CHAPTER 8

CORCORAN LED THEM NORTH TOWARD THE TOWERING RUBY Mountains and the marshes along the eastern flanks of the range. "Figure Humboldt Charley will be heading through that rough country. Treacherous marshes, steep mountains with deep canyons, wolves, mountain lions, and bears, Pappy. That's where we're going."

Fall was telling those around that old man winter was walking close behind. Frost sparkled as the men rode through sage and rabbit brush, tall grass, and scrub cedar. The air was brisk, and the sky was a dark blue as the sunrise made high white clouds sing their beauty.

"My bones are telling me that winter's close, my friend, and you know that Humboldt Charley has those same feelings." Pappy Somerset knew what winter in the Ruby Valley was like. Bitter cold, high winds, and snow measured in feet. "He's gonna be lookin' to hole up somewhere. Got any ideas?"

"There are some nice ranches toward the north, but there's Harrison Pass also that would lead them across the range. Best bet, I guess, would be to keep our eyes open for whatever sign they might have left for us." Corcoran had followed too many outlaws over the last many years and most followed patterns.

"I think that fool will return to what might be called his home place, the Humboldt Wells. That's where his name comes from, and it is wild country with isolated ranches where a gang could ride out a winter."

Steep mountains and broad valleys create strong winter winds and temperatures at twenty below zero are not unusual. "He's gonna want some place that is dry and warm, Pappy, and that area around the old Humboldt Wells could provide that. What we need to do right now is find his trail."

"He's a wily one, Corcoran. Any chance he might just ramble right on through and keep going north? Maybe into Idaho? Wintering in the valley without some kind of protection wouldn't be my first choice."

"Where would you go, Pappy?" Corcoran liked this old army tracker and was going to take every opportunity to learn from him. "My first thought is to where he thinks of as home. What's your thought?"

"He's lived like a wild man in this country for a long time, Corcoran, knows every possible hiding place, every canyon, plateau, river, and spring. That country north of the Wells would offer plenty of game if there was someplace out of the weather. It's wild country, few ranches, deer, antelope, and sage chickens by the gross," he chuckled.

"You thinking of doing something other than Humboldt Charley hunting?" They both chuckled knowing full well they both had those thoughts. Corcoran zeroed in about what Pappy Somerset said about wintering in that country and had to agree. "If Charley had a place, where do you think it might be? I'd take a wild guess and say no more than thirty miles or so away from the new town of Wells."

A community grew up around Humboldt Wells, where the Humboldt River begins, but with the railroad coming through a few miles distant, the community moved and grew alongside the long steel ribbons of commerce.

"Yeah, he's a coon dog. He'd stay close to saloons and whores."

"If you're up to some hard ridin', Pappy, we could angle north east from right here, make it a cross-country ride, no trails, and maybe get to Wells before Humboldt Charley."

"You know the country good enough?" Pappy smiled, egging Terrence Corcoran just a bit. "Wouldn't want to get lost, you know," he chuckled.

"I thought I was lost once," Corcoran laughed. "But I was wrong. It just took me a few extra days to get where I was going. Let's find a good place to camp and we'll head north east when we hit the Ruby Mountains southern boot."

"We can't keep up this pace, Charley," Enos Payson said. "Gonna have dead horses." They rode hard out of Eureka after hitting the bank with guns blazing. "All that gold from Belmont and now more gold from Eureka. These horses are packing too much weight to ride like this much longer."

"I know," Charley snarled. "Sure as hell there's a posse behind us, Payson. It's just the three of us now and I ain't losin' this gold. There's rocks up ahead, big rocks, right where the trail veers off to the Ruby Valley. That mountain range ends in a fortress of rocks. We'll make a stand there. We'll be fightin' like from the walls of a castle, Payson," and he laughed long and hard. "Defending a castle," he howled a couple of times, then very quietly said, "A castle filled with Charley's gold."

It was another hard two miles to those rocks and the three outlaws rode up into the palisades and ramparts, pulled saddlebags and saddles off their worn-out ponies, and hobbled them in some good grass. It took just a matter of moments for the three to set up to fight the posse if there was one. If there was no posse, they'd just enjoy a good rest right along with the horses. Canteens were passed about and shortly after that a flask or two was seen flashing in the cold sunlight.

"Spread out some so they can't concentrate their fire," Buford Gamble hollered. He was down on his belly, his Henry stuck out a crack between two rocks. "I'm looking right down the trail, Charley. I'm gonna kill me a deputy or two."

"Let's kill all the deputies," Charley laughed, finding a good rock to get behind, "then rob us some more banks." He fumbled through his saddlebags, moving bags of gold around and found his flask. "Let's have a nip or two to celebrate our good fortune, boys." They arrived in Belmont as a five-member outlaw gang, lost Spittin' Sam first, then Oliver. Good luck being their shares of the spoils were considerably larger.

"I thought that we hit the jackpot in Belmont," Payson laughed, "until I saw those bags of gold and silver in Eureka. We're getting' kinda proud, boys, when we tell a bank clerk to hold the silver, we don't have room for it."

The three outlaws were laughing and joking like they were on a Sunday picnic in downtown St. Louis as Jimmy Foster led the two townsmen up the trail toward the road that would take them into the Ruby Marshes. "They're riding those horses mighty hard," he said, easily following the trail the gang left. "They ain't tryin' to be sneaky, just running like the cowards they are."

"Be comin' to a rocky area, Foster. They might try to jump us," Giff Blanchard said. "Might want to think about that." Blanchard was near forty, ran a dry goods store and a ranch supply and feed store.

Jimmy Foster was comin' on twenty, vowed he would never be a farmer, didn't cotton to ranching, and took the deputy job when it was offered. "They're hightailing it, Giff. They ain't got no plans to stop. We'll catch 'em tonight when they make camp."

Giff Blanchard shook his head, dropped back a few yards behind the deputy, knowing full well Foster was leading them into an ambush. *Damn fool. Too proud to listen to someone who's been there. Well, Deputy Foster, you get yourself killed and I'll haul your bloody body back to town.*

Sonny Strickland rode up alongside Blanchard, cocked his head to the side a bit. "Does he know about that rocky fortress we're riding toward, Giff? Those rock formations really are a fortress there where the road branches off. Ask any of the old timers about how the Indians used them rocks twenty years ago."

"I warned the pup," Giff Blanchard said. "He don't listen to me anymore than he ever listened to his ma or pa. Why don't you spread out a bit to your left there and I'll git over to my right, and maybe we might live through this chase."

"Dust on the trail," Buford Gamble shouted to Payson and Humboldt Charley. "Looks to be three big brave deputies chasin' us. Let 'em get close, Payson. Don't get trigger happy, there's enough for each of us."

Charley chuckled at Gamble's comment remembering how Enos Payson shot up the Eureka Bank when the clerk dropped his pen. "Yeah, Payson. Wait your turn," he laughed.

Payson grumbled but had to chuckle as they had their fun with him. He too carried a Henry and set himself to kill a deputy. He watched down the long barrel of that fine weapon as the three members of the posse rode in a cloud of late autumn dust. One man was about ten yards or so in front of two others who were flanked well to the sides. "You're mine, Mr. Lead Man," he murmured.

Humboldt Charley and Buford Gamble had the same thoughts as the three rode closer at a comfortable trot. When they were about fifty yards out three rifles belched almost simultaneously and Jimmy Foster's body all but shredded as it was hurled from the saddle and slammed into the desert sand.

Giff Blanchard and Sonny Strickland grabbed their rifles and baled off their horses, rolled to whatever cover they could find, and tried to see where the rifle fire came from. Payson pulled down on Strickland who couldn't get behind anything and put a heavy piece of lead through his head. The outlaws were shooting from high rocks and the flat desert offered little to hide behind.

"Can't see the third man," Gamble said. "You see him, Charley?"

"Yeah," Charley said, quietly. "He's mine." Humboldt Charley moved to his left about ten feet, tucked under a rocky overhang and took a long careful aim. The bullet tore through the top of Giff Blanchard's shoulder as he lay in the sand, forcing a scream from the man. "Got him," Charley whooped.

Blanchard wasn't dead but was about to bleed out. The bullet tore through his lungs, and didn't stop until it found and destroyed Blanchard's liver. The pain only lasted another few seconds and the Eureka merchant was dead.

"We'll give these ponies a good rest," Gamble said. "Payson, see if you can catch a couple of those horses down there. We'll let them carry the saddlebags full of gold and keep all the horses nice and fresh."

"We'll ride north to the railroad and then east to Wells," Charley said. "That little ranch of Maria's is about fifteen miles or so north of there. Let's eat."

"Seagram said his deputy, Foster, lit out after Charley's

gang. That must be these prints we're trailin'. Not many people take this trail and they are fresh. Looks to be three horses, and I know these other prints are from Charley's gang. See that one horse still being rode with a busted shoe." Pappy Somerset and Terrence Corcoran were coming up on the junction where the road would split and the trail to the right would make the turn into the Ruby Valley, and to the left, to Skelton and Elko.

"We'll ride about half a mile toward the Ruby Valley from that turn and then head north east," Corcoran said. They had their horses at a solid trot, eating up the miles when Pappy pulled his horse to a quick stop.

"Look at this, Corcoran," he said, stepping off his horse. They could see where all three horses drew to a fast stop and milled about, saw boot prints and blood. "Here's your deputy," Somerset said, looking at Jimmy Foster's torn up body off to the side of the trail. "Looks like he took three slugs in the middle of his chest."

Corcoran found Giff Blanchard's body and within minutes, Pappy found Sonny Strickland. "They rode straight into an ambush, Pappy. Look at that rock fortress. One of them should have thought about an ambush."

Pappy Somerset shook his head. He knew. "I'll bet that young deputy didn't listen when one of these men warned him. Looks like Humboldt Charley has some extra horse flesh to deal with, too. Let's get these poor bastards buried."

It was more than an hour later they had the posse underground and the area well marked. "Need to shoot something before we make camp tonight, Corcoran. We don't have enough food to keep us to Wells."

Corcoran nodded and mounted up, turning toward the northeast. Wells was probably at least three days away. "Wish we could get word back to Seagram about this. Well, he'll send someone out to find his posse and this is marked well enough, I think."

"Charley has three new horses to carry all that gold, Terrence, but trailing pack animals will slow him down some."

Corcoran just nodded.

CHAPTER 9

It was a fight to get Jeanne Moss to agree to ride to Belmont and see the doctor, but Kleinfelt finally persuaded her. "That ankle isn't just twisted, Jeanne. I think it's broken and only old Doc Patterson would know how to fix it. Leave a note for your hands when they bring the cattle in and let's get going."

"Why isn't the sheriff here?" she demanded, even though she'd been told about him being shot. "And why isn't he leading a posse to find those horrible men? Why are only Pappy Somerset and Corcoran going after those men? You should be out there, Tim Kleinfelt.

"They killed my pa, they shot poor Jeremy, and …" she broke down, crying hard, sobbing and moaning as she remembered what those men did. She stiffened up as her sobs quieted some and her anger returned.

"You should be out there," she all but demanded.

Kleinfelt was more than glad he wasn't riding with Pappy but also wondered if she would be angry the whole ride back to Belmont. "Let's get on the road," he said. "Mr. Jensen, would you ride in the buggy with Jeanne? I think your daughter is about the same age and you'll know what to say and be a help."

Jensen tied his horse to the back of the buggy and put Jeanne's personals in and helped her in. Wrap yourself in this buffalo robe, Jeanne, and we'll make some good time getting back to town."

With one break for rest and food, and another tongue-lashing from Jeanne Moss, Kleinfelt led the party the thirty miles to Belmont, arriving just after sunset. "Well, young lady, you're going to be in good company when I get that ankle straightened out. Your brother is in one bed, the sheriff is in another, but you'll have a room all to yourself." Doc Patterson was rough as hell on the miners and buckaroos who got sick or injured but treated little Jeanne like she was a babe wrapped in soft wool. His old, hard-bitten face, creased and scarred, had an elfish smile, and his eyes were dancing.

"Is it broken?" she asked straight forward. Her days of whimpering were over, and she enjoyed being angry and understood that her anger seemed to get things done.

"No, but it's twisted up something fierce. It'll be tender for some days."

Jeanne asked to see the sheriff when Patterson finished with her ankle and he helped her hobble into his room. "If my father were alive, Sheriff Tetford, he wouldn't be very pleased with the response from your office." Her anger at her treatment by the outlaws, her father's death, and a lack of action from either Tetford or Kleinfelt was well past the boiling point. "The only real response has been from Pappy Somerset and that Corcoran fellow."

"I'm in a cast from my foot to my chest, Jeanne, with my thigh bone, which was sticking out of the skin when they brought me here, held in place with ropes. Tim Kleinfelt is very young and he's the only deputy I have. Most of the men around this old village would rather work on the ranches or the mines than carry an old tin badge.

"Kleinfelt tried to put a posse together and came up with two people and by the time he got to your ranch, he found your brother badly wounded and had to get him back to town. I'm terribly sorry about your loss, Jeanne, but you can't blame anyone but the outlaws. How they treated you is unspeakable and if anyone can catch them, it's Pappy Somerset."

It was slow, but her anger dissipated and she and Tetford talked for about another half hour. "Did you say the man who rode with Pappy was named Corcoran?" Tetford asked.

"That's what he said. Terrence Corcoran. He said he's carried a badge before and was about to start work for the Eureka County sheriff."

"You're sure it was Terrence Corcoran?"

"Yes," she said. She could still see that strong face and those wonderful, soft eyes. She felt like she wanted to run her fingers through his long wavy hair and mess up his big old walrus mustache. "He looked right at me, I was shivering in the cold, my ankle was killing me, with those sad, sad eyes, and said he was there to save me." She was almost in a dream remembering that day.

"If Pappy's riding with Terrence Corcoran then Nevada can say goodbye to Humboldt Charley," Tetford laughed. "If Corcoran knows how badly you were treated, Charley's dead. There's one thing that man won't tolerate and that's mistreatment of women."

By the third day, Fred Seagram was worried enough that he and two others rode north toward the Ruby Marshes to see if they could discover why they hadn't heard anything from either Foster or Corcoran. Seagram's wounded leg made for painful and slow riding, and he spent a great amount of time grumbling. They found the three graves just off the main road near the palisades.

"Sumbitch," Seagram muttered. "Foster, Blanchard, and Strickland, gunned down just like that. Must have been ambushed from the rocks. We'll just have to hope that Corcoran and Somerset can chase those bastards down." Seagram led the men back to Eureka.

"Have Kevin Wombly get these bodies back to town for a decent burial," Seagram said. Wombly was the undertaker in Eureka. "I'll notify the families." Eureka County extended north to the Humboldt River with just the little town of Eureka at the south end and a couple of railroad communities at the north end. Eureka County was mostly rich ranch land peppered with good water and high grass.

The Diamond Valley was an emerald shining with deep grass and plentiful water. Ranches were springing up and fat steers were being brought to market. Most of the crime that Seagram dealt with was stolen stock, territorial fights along water ways, and saloon shenanigans.

"We've got far more cattle than people, but even so, I can't seem to get a decent man to be my deputy. Foster's dead, but he was so young, he really didn't know what he was doing. I've got Corcoran now, but I really don't since he's out chasing Humboldt Charley." He knew that until he heard from Corcoran it would just be him keeping the peace in that little piece of Nevada.

It's time I had a long talk with the county commission about my pay scale, and he chuckled at the thought, rubbing his sore bullet wound. *I bet that banker wished I had a couple of deputies hanging around.*

Seagram sent off telegrams to authorities in Austin, Elko, Winnemucca, Wells, even Virginia City, detailing what had happened in Belmont and Eureka, making everyone aware that Humboldt Charley had a heavy price on his head. "Abusing a young girl and killing an entire posse are the kinds of crimes that will generate a lot of anger toward that fool. I don't care who kills him, I'll consider it completely justified," Seagram said.

"You don't really want to ride right up to the railroad, do you Charley?" Buford Gamble feared that word of their robberies had spread fast and authorities would be on the lookout for the gang.

"No." Charley said. "We'll follow along off to the side of the old wagon road. We'll just look like some old prospectors trailing these ponies. We'll be at Wells in a few days, get supplied and head north to Maria's. We can hole up there for the winter, sit by the fire, and count our gold," he roared with laughter. "I was raised in that country, Buford. Know every inch of it, and we'll be as safe as a babe at mama's teet."

On the second day, they hit the old emigrant trail when they emerged from the Ruby Valley and turned east. They made camp in a copse of cottonwood trees well off the trail. "That was fine shootin', Charley. We'll eat good tonight," Enos Payson said, pulling feathers from a large swan. "Damn fine eatin' too."

"You keep mentioning going to Maria's north of Wells, Charley. Why is it I don't know who you're talking about?" Buford Gamble had been Charley's number one man for two years and couldn't place anyone named Maria.

"She ran a bawdy house in Sheridan, Buford. Remember Consuela's in Sheridan? Her name isn't Consuela, it's Maria Lopez, and she sold that joint and bought a little ranch north of Wells. Runnin' heifers instead of heifers," he laughed hard at his little joke, "And we'll eat well, have plenty of fun too, all winter."

"I remember Consuela's," Payson said. "Does she have some pretty little doves working her cattle?"

The fire was burning bright, there was a good pot of beans boiling away and a full flask of whiskey to be done away before they tucked in. "If she doesn't have a dove or two, we'll pick up a couple in Wells," Charley chuckled. "Only thing we don't want to do is make trouble in Wells. We'll kick up as much crap as we want come spring, but let's keep quiet for the winter, eat good, stay warm, play with the doves, and count our gold."

They laughed and joked until the fire was just embers and the bean pot and flask were empty, and that swan was just bones.

"Should see Wells when we top that ridge, Pappy," Corcoran said. "I'm sure I heard a train whistle last night."

"I think it was the after-effect of your beans, Terrence," Pappy joked. "Do you know the sheriff in Wells?"

"Yup. Dean Whitaker is the town marshal. Known that fat old man for years. Worrisome to the town drunks, hasn't chased an outlaw I know of for a long time. There's more than one who'll tell you he's soft on outlaws, maybe even offering a bit of protection. He won't like it when we tell him Humboldt Charley might be headed his way."

"Will these badges do us any good when we get there?"

"Whitaker might respect 'em," he laughed. "Nobody else will. Lots of traffic through there heading south to Pioche, east to Salt Lake, and west to Elko. Railroad town, too. Gambler's haven, Pappy, and lots of people selling lots of stuff they probably don't own."

"Do you think that Whitaker would let Humboldt Charley spend the winter somewhere around that town? That would sure put us at a disadvantage."

"You bet it would, and some of the things I've heard about Whitaker might make me believe he would if Charley gave him something in return, like not creating trouble in his town.

"They might just need us," Pappy Somerset laughed as the two rode toward a high ridge about three miles in front of them. "I can taste a cold beer all the way out here."

CHAPTER 10

"THAT'S HIM SITTING AT THE FARO TABLE, PAPPY," CORCORAN said, pointing out Wells Town Marshal, Dean Whitaker. "Bet he hasn't walked a mile in a month," he chuckled. "Let's have that beer you were talking about and then ruin the fat man's day."

When they rode into town they put up their horses and took rooms at the Sidewinder Hotel before descending on the marshal's office only to be told the marshal was at the Golden Globe Saloon. The deputy was a snotty little man of about fifty years, skinny and gaunt, white hair that was long, stringy, and hadn't been combed or brushed in half a century. "Don't figger Dean will care much who you are or why you're here," the man said when Corcoran introduced himself.

Wallace Chandler was supposed to be a reformed drunk who also served time for bank robbery and stage coach hold ups during the time the railroads were being built up. He was still a drunk, just not in public. He tolerates Whitaker only because it gets him a bit of change and a place to live. Other than that, Chandler has no use for lawmen.

"You enjoy your little chuckle, deputy, and pass the word

to Whitaker that I'm here. Sure, hope he doesn't pay you much," Corcoran said, tipping his hat with just a touch of a finger.

"A couple of frosty brews, barman," Pappy said when they found some room at the long bar. "And a couple of cigars too."

"Ain't you Terrence Corcoran?" the barman asked, wiping down the bar and pouring the beer. "Name's Lody Sparkman."

"Well now, Lody Sparkman from the Whistle Stop Café in Wadsworth." Corcoran turned to Pappy. "Pappy, I want you to meet one of Nevada's finest barmen, Lody Sparkman. I swear, Lody's poured more than fifteen barrels of beer for me over the years. Life treating you good, old man?"

Sparkman was tall, overweight, and didn't have the least color to his complexion. A barman that never stepped outdoors while the sun was shining. "Got no complaints, Terrence. Nice to meet you, Pappy. If you're riding with Corcoran I have to believe you love a touch of excitement in your life." He looked around and almost whispered, "Who you looking for, Terrence? Should I hope it might be our good town marshal?"

Corcoran laughed at the comment. "No, Lody, not on this visit. Word is that Humboldt Charley might be heading this way. Seen or heard anything 'bout that?"

"Humboldt Charley," he almost stammered. "Whew. Rather not meet up with that wolf and glad to say I ain't heard nothin' 'bout him coming here. I remember when he hit the bank in Winnemucca and raced two posses toward Wadsworth. He took that murdering gang of his right through the Paiute reservation at Pyramid Lake. Damn near started another Indian war, he did.

"Nope, Corcoran, don't want no meeting with that bastard. Marshal Whitaker know anything 'bout that?"

"He will soon's he loses his poke," Corcoran laughed. "Any place in town that has decent victuals, my man?"

"Yup. old Smoky Campbell's opened a joint he calls Beef and Beans over near the railroad station. He and I come to Wells together after he shot up Crandle's place in Wadsworth. Pete Crandle shorted Smoky on a poker table win and won't never short nobody again. 'Course, we had to hightail it out."

Pappy nudged Corcoran and nodded toward the faro table where the rotund Marshal Whitaker was trying to stand up. "Let's spread some bad news, Terrence." They nodded to Sparkman and walked over to the gaming area. Sparkman noticed that Corcoran had unfastened his duster before waking over to the tables.

Man's itching for a fight, it looks like to me. It would be the best thing to happen to Wells if that stupid Whitaker challenges the crazy Irisher.

"Hello, Marshal Whitaker," Corcoran said, offering his hand. "Name's Corcoran, Terrence Corcoran. This here is Pappy Somerset. Can we bend your ear a bit?"

"Corcoran, eh? I've heard of you. If you're here to start trouble, you might just as well ride hard out of town. I don't need no trouble." His voice sounded like it came from the flat side of a dull file scraping steel. High, hard, and shrill, and his belly shook with every breath.

"Me and Pappy are deputy sheriffs from Eureka County, marshal, and we may have some bad news for you." He motioned the marshal to join them at a table and Lody caught his nod to bring some more cold beer. "Humboldt Charley might just be headed this way and you might want to hear me out."

Whitaker had a permanent scowl buried in the puffy rolls of his face, harrumphed a time or two, and sat down. "Humboldt Charley comin' here? I doubt that. I run him and his hog sty gang off more than once."

Pappy saw a slight grin on Corcoran's face and understood that the only thing Whitaker could run off would be an empty place after supper. "Run him off, eh?" Pappy chuckled. "Well, we don't plan to run him off, marshal. We're lookin to run him in, dead or alive." Pappy had a satisfied look on his face and took a long sip of beer.

"He robbed the bank in Belmont, killed some people in the process, and just a few days ago robbed the bank in Eureka, killed the posse that chased him. He's lookin' to winter up, and he may be comin' here to do it. Heard he has a hidey hole north of here."

Whitaker swilled his glass of beer, stood up, and marched out, saying, "He ain't comin' here and you got no reason to stay, Corcoran. I'll crush you like a pimple on my ass if you start trouble." Glasses rattled with each footfall from the large marshal as he stomped out of the saloon.

"I like a man with kindness and warmth in his soul," Pappy Somerset chuckled. "Got a plan, Corcoran?"

"Yup. Let's check out Smoky's Beef and Beans, get a good night's sleep, and do some ridin' around tomorrow. See what we can find."

"You mean you're not gonna let that mean old marshal run you out of town? Well my goodness," Pappy chortled, hearing guffaws from Corcoran. "Looks to be a cold fall, Corcoran. If that means an early winter, we go to catch that bandito." Corcoran lifted an eyebrow, questioning that statement.

"I've got winter wood cut and split in Belmont, Corcoran, and a stone fireplace to burn it in. I don't intend to be wasting hearth time chasing Humboldt Charley." They were laughing and joshing stepping into Smokey's Beef and Beans.

"I ain't never had a piece of beef that tough, Corcoran. A

ten-year-old bull can't be that tough. Let's break our fast at the hotel café instead of Smoky's joint."

"Gotta say, though, them beans were good," Corcoran laughed. "My teeth hurt." They walked out on the main street of Wells just about the time the sun made itself known. The little town serviced ranches spread out in all directions, was a main stop for the intercontinental railroad, and had a thriving commercial neighborhood.

Commercial buildings lined the main street, some as much as three stories tall, benefitting from the railroad. Moving the community from the emigrant trail at Humboldt Wells to where the railroad passed was a success for all concerned. "Plenty of hotel space and many gambling tables at the saloons must keep this town hopping," Corcoran mused.

"People moving around early, Terrence," Pappy said. "I like that."

Corcoran wondered if all these people were up early or had stayed up late. He was chuckling as they walked back up on the boardwalk and into the hotel café for breakfast. They headed for an open table near the front window when a slight, redheaded tornado flung herself at Corcoran.

"Terrence," she howled with delight. "I've missed you," she wailed, hugging him, trying her best to kiss him right on the mouth. Twenty-five breakfast guests took in the scene, some with pleasure, some not.

"Angie Bonét," he said, quietly, enjoying the hug, her body pressed firmly to his. "It's been some time, pretty lady." He let her have her way for another moment or two and then untangled from the embrace. "I like a warm welcome when I come to town, don't you Pappy? Say hello to Angie."

Pappy just stood there, smiling, looking around at the crowded café, shook Angie's hand, and took his seat. *This man must know everyone in the state of Nevada, and every woman for certain. In a way, I hope we have to chase old Humboldt Charley through another five or six towns.*

Angie Bonét was from New Orleans originally and came to Nevada by way of San Francisco and Sonora in California. "You're a singer and dancer, Angie. What are you doing here?" Corcoran asked. He was enjoying letting his eyes roam about a small but fine figured woman.

Angie was probably closing in on the forty mark, but was in excellent physical condition. Her face was finely chiseled with a sharp nose, wide and soft brown eyes, and tender lips that cried for attention. Her red hair cascaded well below her shoulders when she flounced them about some.

"My troupe broke up on our last tour, Terrence. Right after we played in Virginia City. I could either sing and dance in saloons or work as a dove. I chose neither and bought this little café." Her smile dazzled Corcoran and Somerset, and the male patrons at all the other tables. She flung her arms wide, taking in the many tables and patrons.

"You made the right choice, little darlin'," Corcoran said. "Pappy, this charming lady actually had me dancing on the stage at Piper's Opera House in Virginia City one night. I ruined her feet, stomping all over them," he laughed.

"Oh, no, Terrence Corcoran. You're a fine dancer. If fact, if you're going to be in town for a few days, there's a public dance at the rail worker's hall Saturday night. Will you dance with me?"

"I wouldn't miss it, Angie love," he said, nodding at the tables around him, getting a few envious smiles from the men folk and a few frowns from the women. Angie Bonét would be a perfect fit in New Orleans or San Francisco, but not quite in Wells.

They were on the road in an hour, traveling north to look at some of the ranches. "If Charley is looking to winter-up around here, he'll need a ranch that doesn't have a lot of stock, a lot of hired hands, and is damn remote," Corcoran said. "Not so remote that a man couldn't ride into town and get back easily in a day."

"This is open country, Terrence, but I remember some rolling hills dotted with pines and cedar some twenty miles northeast of here. Ramrodded a road crew that needed someone what could read terrain. A couple of ranches in the area," Pappy said. "I know there was water and the ranches had good grass."

"Lead on, Mr. Somerset. You da boss," he chuckled. It was a cold morning for this early in the season and they were bundled up in their heavy coats and scarves wrapped around their necks. Corcoran wore a heavy buffalo robe coat that he picked up the Black Hills years ago. "Might be an early winter coming on," he said.

"We'll pick up some supplies in Wells and head north, Gamble," Charley said. "We'll be here through the winter, but we'll just get some stuff to make Maria happy."

"We better be here long enough for some cold beer and hard whiskey," Enos Payson said. "My flask ran empty early yesterday."

"Mine too," Charley laughed. "We'll fill our bellies, fill our flasks, and pick up a jug or two. That's what I meant by supplies," he said. There were many eyes on the group as they rode down the main street, laughing and talking loud. Charley loved to make a scene and was unhappy and grumpy if he didn't. They tethered all six of their horses in front of the Golden Globe and sauntered in to the smoke-filled emporium of good times.

The saloon was filled with locals and visitors, smoke hanging heavy in the air, the smell of spilled whiskey and warm bodies mingling with the smoke. Many eyes turned toward the three men coming through the bat-wing doors.

Humboldt Charley, Buford Gamble, and Enos Payson turned immediately toward the long bar.

"Whoa up there, injun," a loud voice said as they sauntered toward the bar. "You just high-tail it right on out of here." The man was large, broad through the chest and shoulders, carried a Peacemaker and had his right hand mighty close to it. His face was scarred from his left eye down across his lips and chin from a knife fight many years ago, his eyes were almost black with anger and hate, and he carried a badge to boot. Wayne "Scar" Figgins was another former outlaw who carried a badge in Wells.

Figgins was a cattle rustler and bank robber out of Texas and New Mexico, did time at the federal penitentiary in Huntsville, and ran roughshod over the saloon patrons in Wells. Many gamblers and saloonkeepers slipped some gold coins the marshal's way to keep Figgins under control.

"Injuns don't drink with white folk in this town," Deputy Marshal Wayne Figgins snarled. "Turn it around and get it out the door, and I won't say it again."

Humboldt Charley turned his head slightly, as if to follow orders, whirled, and his gun belched fire twice, sending "Scar" Figgins crashing into a table. Not dead yet, Figgins was pulling iron when a rifle slug tore half his head off. Charley, Payson, and Gamble were on their ponies and out of town before Marshal Dean Whitaker was out of his chair.

"You'll learn one of these days not to wear that damn feather in your hat, Charley," Payson said as they pushed their horses on the north road at a full gallop.

"I'm half Paiute and damn proud of it, Enos. Ain't no badge carrying sumbitch tell me I can't drink where I want." He laughed hard. "I drink where I want and when I want, and nobody tells me I can't."

"Well, that one won't," Gamble laughed, getting Charley laughing, too. "We're about fifteen miles from Maria's, boys.

Let's slow these ponies down some so we don't have to walk in."

The road north was through rolling hills covered in pine, cedar, sage, and rabbit brush, along with plenty of grasses, prime country for cattle, deer, and antelope, and sparsely populated with people. Maria's place was tucked about three miles east of the road, down in a little valley. The trail in wandered through thick stands of piñon, deep arroyos carved by centuries of spring run-off and summer thunderstorms, and rock escarpments poised as sentries.

"We don't want to bring a posse down on her, Gamble," Charley said as they trotted their horses north. "Let's split up and ride all zig-zag cross-country for a couple of hours, working our way toward the ranch. Make it hard for a posse to follow, and if somebody does get close, kill 'em.

"It's gettin' late and they won't want to try to follow us once it gets dark," Charley laughed. "Like the chickens, they gotta be nested up at dark," and he rode off toward the east through the brush and trees. The others split into different directions, keeping their horses at a good trot, eating miles of desert. It was a cold day with the wind blowing in from the northwest, cold, and filled with the threat of an early snow.

CHAPTER 11

"You're right, Pappy, we gotta take a good close look at that one little ranch you showed me. You said it was tucked away in that valley, which means it isn't visited often. Whoever has that place has good grass, good water, and it would sure as hell be easy to protect. We'll ride back in the morning and make camp where we can see the place. It would be ideal for Humboldt Charley."

"What stood out in my mind, Corcoran, there were so few cattle and horses. This time of year, there should have been a large herd of cattle being brought down from the high country, and we should have seen a lot of activity. We gotta keep our eye on that place."

The ranchers in the area drove cattle to the railroad yards in Wells and Halleck for shipment east and west, but not from that ranch, apparently. "Without creating any interest from anyone, let's see if we can find out who owns or runs that property," Pappy said.

"We rode a pretty fair circle today, Pappy, and we haven't seen another person or dust from one. Maybe Whitaker doesn't have to protect outlaws. Maybe they ain't nobody around to give a damn about 'em." They chuckled about that some feeling the cold of evening coming on.

The sun was almost down as Pappy Somerset and Terrence Corcoran rode into Wells and up to the livery. "Howdy Sam," Corcoran said to the stable hand. "Been a long day for these critters. Feed 'em good, will you? And we'll be leaving out early in the morning, probably with our mule, too."

"You missed all the action, Corcoran," Sam said, holding Rube and Pappy's horse. "Looks like some wild Indian wanted a drink real bad and killed the deputy when he wouldn't let him in the saloon. Crazy bastards, aren't they?"

"Anybody with that crazy Indian?"

"Yup," Sam said. "Two mean looking guys. All three rode out of town fast. Marshal Whitaker's out with a posse now. One thing, Corcoran. They each had a pack animal with them. Unusual for three men ridin' together to each have a pack animal. Must be carrying more than trail needs."

Corcoran had to chuckle that the stable owner would pick up on that. "Yup, Sam," he said. "They be carrying something more than side meat and beans."

"That must have been that one bit of dust we saw," Pappy said. "Didn't happen to get a good look at that crazy Indian, did you, Sam?"

"Dressed like a cowboy but had a big old feather stuck in his sombrero, and wore laced up high moccasins. He was an ugly one," Sam chuckled.

Corcoran and Somerset nodded to each other and headed for the Golden Globe for some cold beer. "Humboldt Charley got here while we were out, Pappy. They gotta hole up now. Killin' a deputy in a town that seems to give them protection? They gotta hide somewhere. We'll get 'em."

"Bet fat old Whitaker will be on the war path," Somerset

chuckled. "I don't think I want to watch that man sitting on a trotter."

Corcoran blew beer out his nose and bit his cigar in half seeing vividly what Pappy said. "My gawd, that would be a sight." He was doubled over laughing. "Poor dumb horse, too," and Pappy joined him in loud laughter.

"You boys are having some fun," Lody Sparkman said, setting a couple more beers down and wiping up the mess Corcoran made. "Hear about our little shoot-out in here?"

"Man at the stables just told us. It was Humboldt Charley, for sure?" If anyone in Wells could identify Charley it would be Lody Sparkman after the dealings he had with the man back in Wadsworth. When you're up close and personal with a man threatening to blow your head off, you tend to remember what he looks like.

"Sure, as hell was, Corcoran. I'll never forget that face. He put two slugs into Scar Figgins faster than anything I've ever seen before. Whitaker'll never find 'em," Sparkman chuckled. "Think you will?"

"That's what we're here for," Pappy said. "That bad man's days are numbered." He was about to say more when they heard a group of horses' ride past the saloon. "Looks like the town marshal has returned."

"Seems as though we were in the wrong place at the wrong time, Pappy. Never occurred to me that we should have stayed in town today." He just shook his head, downing the beer.

Corcoran and Somerset joined a few others from the bar at the large windows and looked out onto the street where Marshal Dean Whitaker was being helped off his horse by a couple of members of the posse. A couple of others had their backs turned on purpose, doing their best not to be seen snickering.

"Think the fat man was shot?" Pappy asked.

One of the onlookers chuckled. "Hell no, he ain't been shot. He's so fat he needs help gittin' on his horse, and cain't git off without help. Some say he's always lookin' down at you from his high horse," and the man laughed right out loud.

"Take a mighty big bullet to get through all that and then do damage," Corcoran laughed, holding his belly as if it was a large bowl of pudding. "Let's go see what we can learn."

They sauntered across the dusty street to where Whitaker was standing. "Make contact with Charley?" Corcoran asked. He wanted to say something like, 'if you'd listened to me you would have been prepared,' but simply asked the kind of question that would anger the man.

"Get out of my way Corcoran, this is my jurisdiction." He was limping as two posse members helped him onto the boardwalk and into his office.

Corcoran ambled over to where the two posse members that had been chuckling stood. "Whitaker get himself shot?" he asked.

The tall lean one snickered, chewed some on a cigar stub and looked Corcoran and Pappy up and down. "Horse tripped, and he fell off," the cowboy said.

"Bounced twice," his partner said, and the two walked off toward the Golden Globe, hee-hawing and whacking each other on the back.

"Must have been a sight worth seein'," Pappy laughed. "We must have missed a good ride, Terrence."

"I'm wondering if we might be able to follow their trail come sunup," Corcoran said as they walked into the café for supper. "Humboldt Charley has never been caught because he's one smart sumbitch. But, you my friend, are known from Powder River to Adobe Wells as one fine tracker. If we can pick up Charley's trail in the morning, we might get an idea of where he'll winter up."

"Yup," is all Pappy Somerset said as Angie Bonét walked up and slipped a hand on his shoulder and smiled at Corcoran.

"You boys got some trail dust on ya," she said. "A platter of slow smoked brisket smothered in my Cajun sauce might just let you sleep good tonight."

"A warm Cajun princess cuddled up close might keep a man awake all night, too," Corcoran whispered, gently slipping an arm around her full hips. She didn't push the arm away and gave the big man a generous smile.

"This princess might enjoy her knight in dusty buckskin if she thought he might stick around for more than a few days."

"Cain't never tell, now can you?" he chuckled.

Sunrise found the men riding north out of the bustling railroad town, trailing a mule, and smiles on their faces. "Wasn't sure you'd be up and about this morning, Terrence. Must have been a busy night for you."

"Oh, Pappy, it was a pleasant night after all the preliminary fireworks."

"I knew you had powerful arms and shoulders, Corcoran, but I don't think I've ever seen a man hit as hard as you hit that sniveling little deputy. You lifted him clean over that table," Somerset chuckled.

"I don't like to beat up on another law dog, Pappy, but that man just heated my juices some, calling me prideful. It wasn't me that said those things about me, it was Lody, and then Angie. Why, my heavens, Pappy, I don't ever talk about myself like that. Prideful, he called me."

"Well, that, and a few other choice names," Pappy laughed. "You are aware that he went for his gun, aren't you? Just before you broke his jaw? Sent him flying through the rarefied air?" Pappy was laughing hard as he said all these things and Corcoran just rode old Rube quietly along, grinning some, chewing on a cigar.

"If you was a deputy marshal here, and one of the other deputy marshals in the office got himself shot and killed by Humboldt Charley, would you try to defend Charley's actions? Why would that prune face deputy say what he did?"

"I don't know, Corcoran. Whitaker is more interested in getting you out of town than he is worrying that one of his deputies was killed. And this deputy, old Wallace Chandler says the one that was killed was out of line."

"If Whitaker is protecting Charley," Corcoran snarled, "I'll render every drop of fat from his grotesque body just before I shoot him. I shot a sheriff, you know. I ain't afraid of shooting a deputy marshal."

"You shot a sheriff?"

"I'll tell you the story some time," Corcoran chuckled. "Let's see where Charley leads us."

"I want to know what went on after you and Angie were dancing to that piano and banjo music." Corcoran just continued smiling and nudged Rube into a nice trot.

It was easy following the tracks of the posse out of town and about an hour out they found where the group had stopped and let their horses just mill about some. "Probably where Whitaker fell off," Corcoran said. Pappy stepped off his horse and handed the reins to Corcoran.

"Don't think so," he said after walking around the outside perimeter of where the activity was. "Come down here and look at this. I love to find things like this," Pappy said. Corcoran stepped off and tied the horses and mule to a large sage.

Pappy walked Corcoran around the area, pointed out several different things in three locations. A time or two he almost got down on his knees to look closely at some prints in the dirt and dust. "See what they missed?"

"You're just as good as the legend says you are," Corcoran smiled. "So, Charley and the two others milled about for a short time, right here, and then rode off in three different directions. Why didn't Whitaker follow?"

"Never saw the obvious prints to follow," Somerset said. "But I do."

"It just dawned on me that I do too, Pappy. You pointed out those prints to me twice before. Damn me. There are three horses being ridden and three more trailed, but one set of prints easier to see and follow than any of the others. That dumb bastard is gonna wish he'd taken care of his horse and got that shoe fixed."

Pappy led them off through the brush and desert following a horse with a broken shoe. "We said it before, Corcoran. They should have had that shoe fixed. Glad they didn't."

"Maria, my love," Humboldt Charley smiled, wrapping his arms around the lovely lady. Maria Consuela Lopez Gonzales, called Maria, owned a large ranch about thirty miles north of Wells and welcomed visits by men like Humboldt Charley. They paid well to stay there for periods of time, protected by the remoteness of the ranch and by its natural defense, sitting in a basin. One couldn't ride into that basin without being seen from the ranch house.

The low rim rock that surrounded the basin was mostly void of heavy brush and virtually no trees grew in the rocks. A small creek meandered through the valley and as it left the valley on the west, it harbored the only trail in. If the rim rock were higher and if the valley were narrower, it might almost be considered a box canyon.

"My compadres will be joining me later and we would like to spend some time with you. Maybe most of the winter." He gathered her into his powerful arms, let one hand give her generous bottom a nice friendly pat, and received a long, wet kiss from the lady.

"You know my rules, Charley," she smiled, rubbing her body slowly against his. "Don't bring the law down on this place and pay me well. You have gold?" Maria, as most called her, was about five feet five and one hundred thirty pounds or so. She was flirtatious, willing if the price was right, and feisty as a bobcat.

Some in Elko County believed that she led some of the gangs since it was believed that she had been seen at Winnemucca bank holdups, Elko County cattle rustling scenes, and danced with many law officers at public gatherings. Corcoran had heard these rumors about Maria Lopez but had no idea where she lived or how much of the stories should be believed.

"Ah, my little vixen, I have gold and you will be paid well. I was going to bring you some bottled gifts from Wells, but couldn't. How about fixing me a drink while I take care of my horse?"

"You can stay in the second bedroom Charley. How many friends are with you? They can stay in the bunkhouse."

Charley told her two would be here soon and he walked out to put his horses in the barn, out of sight. He brought his bedroll, pack, and heavy saddlebags into the large bedroom that featured a separate outside entrance. The ranch house was built in the Colonial Spanish way, with a long corridor off the main rooms that led to bedrooms, each with an outside door to a covered porch. Ranch kilned brick, heavy timber, and lots of tile were included in the building.

Charley pulled five double eagles from the bags and handed them to Maria when he walked back into the large great room. She handed him a glass of whiskey and a lit cigar.

"Nice," she said, enjoying the weight of the coins. They sat

CHAPTER 12

"Does this fool have any idea where he's going or what he's doing?" Corcoran and Pappy had been following the horse with the broken shoe for hours through thick sage, along sloping side hills, into deep arroyos, and through thick stands of forest. "I'm just a bit confused by all this." The wind had picked up and along with that the temperature had fallen dramatically.

"This is an old Indian trick, Corcoran. I've only actually seen it once before. Three warriors raid a village, steal something, and light out. They know they'll be followed so they split up and then just wander around for hours. The posse gave up right away. Too soon in my opinion.

"Of course, if you're right and Whitaker protects people like Humboldt Charley, then stopping the chase early would have been planned. But, as you are already thinking this is a wild goose chase, you can see how effective this is. If it weren't for that distinctive horse shoe, we would have lost them."

"So, you're saying these tracks will lead us somewhere, eventually? I better remember some of this stuff you're crammin' in my old head bone." He chuckled thinking that it wasn't that long ago that he thought he knew something about tracking outlaws. *This old man has forgotten more about trackin' than I'll ever know. What I like is that he's so casual about it.*

"If you've been paying attention, Mr. Corcoran, sir, this fool, as you call him, is slowly working his way toward that ranch we saw yesterday. I will bet you the cost of a cold beer that we stumble on other tracks within the next couple of hours, and they will end up at that ranch."

Corcoran liked to think of himself as a man who could get the job done and for several hours visions of Jeanne Moss had been dancing in his head and he wasn't getting the job done, wasn't whipping the tar out of the men who ravaged the girl, and instead, was simply taking a leisurely trail ride through the desert.

Ain't my idea of tracking down an outlaw. On the other hand, Pappy ain't been wrong about anything so far. All right then, this plan, if you call it that, must really work. I would have been ready to give up, figurin' I wasn't really following an outlaw, just like the posse give up. Well, damn, Terrence, me boy, you just learned something. Another 'Great Truth' on this path of life.

Pappy heard Corcoran chuckle but didn't say anything.

The country they were riding through was typical Great Basin landscape, with steep rocky mountain ranges separated by fertile valleys filled with sage, piñon, cedar, and grasses. Most of eastern Nevada was excellent cattle country and many large ranches were springing up regularly.

They rode east into rolling foothill country out of a large open valley, following two horses, one with a broken shoe. "It's strange, Pappy, that Whitaker wasn't able to catch these fools. They rode into Wells, each trailing a packhorse that they stole from the posse they killed. They killed a deputy and ran off.

"Three outlaws, each trailing a packhorse, aren't gonna be

able to out run a damn old posse, Pappy." Corcoran was getting more and more angry about everything that had happened. A lawman who might be helping a murderous gang, a trail he was following that wasn't going anywhere, and the thoughts of little Jeanne Moss being so horribly abused by those bastards.

"I swear Pappy, I'm gonna kill 'em three times each."

"Recognize that little rise in front of us, Corcoran? Off to your right just a couple of degrees. See that road that climbs up and over that rise? We were there yesterday." Corcoran spotted the road going over the top of the saddleback ridge and saw the great stands of piñon pine along the hillside's flanks.

"Yup. We crawled through those trees and spent some time looking down on that little ranch, and this trail we're following will take us right there. By damn, Pappy, you really know your stuff.

"We sure don't want to ride right up there. Let's circle down south some and come up on that little vale from the southeast. I don't remember seeing a road or trail in that area. We want to see them and not let them see us."

"That's a small little valley the ranch sits in, so there will be a hillside of some kind if we circle around to it." Pappy Somerset was looking off to his right and smiled as he pointed at the ground. "Looky here, Corcoran. Another rider just joined up with old busted shoe."

"Just like you said he would," Corcoran smiled. "I'm glad we brought the pack mule. We might be here for a few days depending on what we find. One thing's for sure, it's gonna storm and soon, I think." The wind had a winter's bite to it and far to the northwest they could see clouds that towered into the stratosphere.

"Old Charley's gonna be holed up in a warm ranch house and we're gonna be tucked into a camp in cold rock canyon," Pappy laughed, nudging his horse into a nice fast walk.

It was late in the afternoon before Terrence Corcoran and Pappy Somerset were slowly climbing up a steep, rock-strewn hillside, sparsely covered in brush and scrub cedar. "We'll use that rocky ridge to hide us when we get to the top," Pappy said. "Should be able to look right down on that ranch."

They were running out of daylight but wanted to see something down below before they thought about setting up a camp. "We saw those hoof prints on that road, so at least we know those horses went toward the ranch," Corcoran chuckled. "Let's hope it's one of the outlaws on that horse." Pappy gave him a sour look as if to say, 'you know it is.'

They came to the saddleback of the ridge and eased behind some large rock formations to look down on the little valley. For being late in the fall, the grass was high and thick and there weren't any cattle taking advantage of it. They could see smoke curling up from the house chimney, and saw one man in a corral, working on a horse's hooves.

Corcoran pulled his telescope out and extended the tube for a look into that corral. "Fixin' a broken shoe, Pappy." He handed the glass to Somerset. "Now all we gotta do is figure out who is doing the fixin'. I've seen Charley, but I've only heard about others that ride with him."

"Don't recognize him, Corcoran. Let's go make camp and we'll get closer tomorrow. Maybe even shoot somebody." They laughed, slipping down out of sight. "Gonna be cold tonight, I think. Might even have some wind to make it nasty."

"It's a breeze until it hits about thirty miles an hour, then it's a wind. It will be breezy tonight," Corcoran joshed as they crawled back down the hillside to their horses to ride off about a mile to set up camp. "We spent enough time in the saddle today to qualify for a buckaroo's job, Pappy, and ended up right where we thought we would even if it took an extra twenty miles or so to get here."

"Yup," is all Pappy said, and they mounted up to find a camp.

They were nestled in a stand of pine and cottonwood trees with a spring spreading its bounty into a pool about four feet across. "We'll keep our fires small and make no smoke, Terrence. We should be plenty far enough away that they won't spot us."

Angie Bonét had packed several pounds of smoked and dried meat, bacon, some hard tack, and plenty of coffee for the camp. Corcoran used the canvas from the pack to put up a lean-to while Pappy dug a small fire pit and made it deeper by piling rocks around the hole. "Nice little home we have, Pappy," Corcoran laughed as he brought in an armload of dried wood. "Maybe spend the winter, eh?"

"Those boys better either be dead or in chains a long time before winter, Mr. Corcoran, sir. But it will be chilly around here in the mornings."

"Chilly I can handle," Corcoran said. "Marrow-deep freezing cold is something else."

"Think old Whitaker will be put out for killin' that deputy?" Buford Gamble was wolfing a platter of side meat and fresh eggs Maria placed on the table. It was a brilliant late fall morning, sunlight splashing through open windows, and a light breeze wafting about. "I got no trust in that fat man. He'd sell you out in a minute."

"Ain't nobody been following us since we stole that girl Buford, so there ain't nobody to pay old Whitaker," Charley laughed long and hard at his little joke. Buford didn't think it was funny. "He don't do nothin' less'n he gets paid, dead deputy or not. What's more, I don't give a damn how upset he might get."

"I hope you're right. I'm gonna take a little ride around Maria's place this morning and make sure we ain't been followed. Just ain't right that we robbed two banks, killed a bunch of folks, and only that little posse out of Eureka has chased after us."

"What's this world comin' too, eh Buford?" Charley thought that was one of the funniest things he'd ever said. "Come on, Maria, let's go make that old mattress of yours beg for mercy." She giggled, took a poke at Buford, and let Humboldt Charley lead her down the long hallway to her bedroom.

"Man thinks he's invincible," Buford grumbled, swilling the last of his coffee. He walked out to the barn to saddle his horse. "Mornin' Payson," he said to his riding partner. "It's a cold one today even with the sun shining. Get that horse of yours taken care of?"

"He'll be sore for a day or two, but got new shoes on him. Goin' somewhere?" Buford had pulled his horse from a stall and was brushing him out.

"Charley doesn't think Whitaker or anyone else has followed us, but I want to make sure. Just gonna ride around a bit."

"Whitaker's too old and fat to worry about," Payson said. "Ain't had the slightest thought of anyone else might be trailing us. I'm gonna nurse a bottle of whiskey, watch the sky for signs of winter, and sleep some. You make sure we're good and safe, Buford," he said with a wry snicker.

"Asshole," Buford snarled, throwing a blanket and saddle on his horse. He could hear Payson chuckling all the way across the broad expanse to the ranch house. "You boys won't be laughing if I find somebody's been trailing us." He rode out of the barn, sitting tall and straight, toward the road they came in on, changed his mind, and decided to ride southeast toward a rim-rock ridge half a mile or so out.

A few men with rifles could sit up in those rocks and pick us off, easy. I gotta have a long talk with old Charley. Between Payson's bein' dumb and Charley's thoughts not bein' on livin' long, means I'm in somebody's sights. And we got a bedroom full of gold. Damn.

"That's what I call a sunrise, Pappy. Look at those colors." Corcoran had a fire going, coffee almost boiling, and was cutting some bacon strips for their cast iron frying pan. "Can't have one of these good cookin' pans unless you have a pack mule to carry it," he chuckled. "Ever made biscuits in one of these, Pappy?"

"You think you and the bears are the only ones what craps in the woods, boy? I been making biscuits in cast iron pans for fifty years." He had his shirt tucked in and boots pulled on, poured both of them some coffee and gave Corcoran the idea that he might even do a little jig around the camp.

"You're full of it this morning," Corcoran laughed. "I got a good feelin' about what we're gonna find today. Watching that old boy shoe that horse was the right thing to see. Every time I think about what those men did to little Jeanne, my blood boils."

"What she went through will be in the back of her mind for the rest of her life, Corcoran. She's a strong one, though. Her pa, old Bill Moss was as tough a man as I ever knew, and he raised her like he would a boy. She does a man's work around that ranch. If we don't kill Humboldt Charley, it would not surprise me if she took up the chase."

They ate their bacon, soaked some hard tack in coffee and bacon grease, and saddled up for the ride back to that rocky overlook. The morning was cold but a clear sky and bright sun warmed things up nicely. "No wind, breeze, or tornado this morning. Maybe that storm's gonna hold off for a day or two."

With their horses tied off at the base of the hill, they crawled up to the outcrop of rock. Smoke could be seen coming from a kitchen stove, but no movement around the corrals or pastures. "Strange way to run a cattle ranch, Corcoran. No cattle, no cowboys, no movement just after sunrise."

"I wonder who owns that little place? It's set up to be a fair operation, Pappy. If I were a settlin'-down type I might just want something like that."

"Somebody's moving," Pappy said.

Corcoran got his glass out and watched Enos Payson come out of what he figured was the bunkhouse and walk to the barn. "Same man we saw yesterday shoeing his horse." He handed the glass to Somerset. "Still don't recognize him."

"Looks like somebody comin' out of the main house and heading to the barn, too," Pappy said, watching Buford Gamble walk across the wide yard. "I've seen this one before."

Corcoran took the long glass and put it to his eye. "Yeah, me too," he snarled. "That's Buford Gamble, a back-shootin' sumbitch if there ever was one. Chased him when I was working near Silver City up in Idaho several years ago. Wonder when he tangled up with Humboldt Charley? Charley's insane, you know."

"Sounds like those two would make a serious pair. I've heard Buford's name and he looks familiar, but I don't know why." He kept his eye on the barn for another minute. "I know where I've seen him. He was in Belmont the morning the bank was robbed. Had coffee at the San Francisco Café and left out when old Bill Moss came in. I'll bet he took word of Moss bringing his army money to the bank to Charley's camp outside town."

"You've got a good memory, Pappy. Looks like Gamble's gonna take a little horseback ride," Corcoran said. They watched Buford Gamble ride toward the main road then turn and ride in their general direction. "This might be interesting," he chuckled.

Enos Payson walked into the kitchen and poured a cup of coffee, taking a seat at the large rough-cut table. Anna Rosales walked in, smiled and said hello. "And, hello to you, lovely girl. Are you cooking breakfast?" Payson couldn't take his eyes off the beautiful teenager as she poured herself some coffee.

Her blouse was such that she could wear it off her shoulders which gave Payson a good look at her filled out figure. She wore a long skirt, tight in the waist and hips and flared from her thighs. Her hair, so black it shone cobalt, hung long and in waves, cascaded to her hips. Her smile was helped by bright lively eyes that sparkled in the early morning light.

"I guess I could," she smiled, pouring some coffee into Payson's cup too. "Maria or Ricardo usually does the cooking, but I can fix you up."

Payson thought he was sure she could fix him up and wanted to grab her up and run to the bunkhouse. "How about some bacon and eggs and then maybe you and me could get together and have a little fun. You like to have fun?"

She gave him a look out of the side of her face, a hint of a smile playing on her sensuous mouth. "Sure. I like to have fun," she said. She ran her hand across the back of his shoulders as she took the coffee pot back to the stove. A nervous shudder ran down his back. His eyes lit up and he knew he had just been given the okay to do as he pleased with the girl.

"You got some spirit in you, girl. I like that. Ain't nobody around cept'n us, so let's not waste any time." He chortled when she nudged right up against him, letting him feel the fullness of her young body.

Payson pulled her onto his lap, letting his hands roam freely about her lithe body. Sun was streaming through the kitchen windows and he eased her onto the floor, kissing her hard on the mouth. She worked her hips hard into his and he responded back, groaning in pleasure.

She squealed with joy, wrapping her arms around him and letting his mouth come to hers. They bumped the table about, the chair was scratching on the wooden floor as they rubbed their bodies together, harder and faster. They were making a racket in their playfulness, groaning, laughing, thumping about.

Enos Payson was about to get his pants unfastened when a bullet tore through the middle of his back, blasted through his chest, and cleaved through Anna's chest. The echoes of the rifle shot were still rumbling when the two bodies fell apart from each other on the floor, blood flowing freely. Maria Lopez stood at the doorway with a smoking Henry rifle in her hands. Humboldt Charley was running up the corridor trying to get his pants fastened.

"What the hell have you done?" he howled. Looking at the mess on the floor, even Humboldt Charley was able to understand what was going on just before that single shot rang out.

"I told you that I would kill any man who put his hands-on Anna, Charley. I told you I would do that, and I have." She slumped in a chair, the Henry fell from her hands and clattered to the floor, and she wept, saying the girl's name over and over.

CHAPTER 13

"Looks like Buford Gamble is gonna ride that pony right up the side of this old hill and plop himself down at our feet, Pappy." Gamble rode at a quiet walk, taking in the surrounding countryside, looking for any kind of man-made sign. The slightest movement, a boot print or horse whinny, and he would have hightailed it back to the ranch or pulled his weapon and killed.

"If we shoot him, it'll bring the gang down on us," Pappy whispered. "We got to knock him out of the saddle and knife him or whack him with a rock."

"If he rides close, we'll do that. You knock him out of the saddle, I'll do the rest," Corcoran said. Gamble had his eyes moving constantly, at the ground in front, across the face of the rim-rock ridge, in the trees scattered about. He was riding straight at Pappy who was ready to leap at the man when there was a gunshot from the ranch house.

"What the hell?" Gamble said, turning his horse and putting it in a full gallop back to the ranch.

"Maybe we won't have to kill 'em, Pappy," Corcoran laughed, watching Gamble ride hard down the rocky hill. "They'll do themselves in." They settled in behind some rocks watching the ranch. "Jeanne told us there were three men, Sheriff Seagram said three men robbed the bank, and we followed three riders with three pack horses.

"If that gunshot means what I hope it does, the odds are even."

"That is, if there aren't fifteen men inside that ranch house counting all the gold Humboldt Charley brought in. No, Terrence, we have to assume there are people there besides Charley and his gang."

"Best way to know how many are there will be to count horses," Corcoran said. "Charley arrived with six horses. I'll sneak into the barn tonight and count horses and we'll know what we're up against."

"Look at this now," Pappy said, pointing down at the area between the house and the barn. "That's Humboldt Charley and Buford Gamble." Pappy had the telescope to his eye and Corcoran scrambled around a large rock to get a better view. "Gamble's carrying a bloody body, Terrence. A girl's body.

"My God, Terrence, they've killed a young girl."

"What the hell's Charley doing? I can't make it out from here."

Pappy brought the long glass around, so he could see the ranch house porch. "He's dragging another body out. One shot and two dead? Who's that helping Charley?" He handed the telescope back to Corcoran.

"I don't recognize her, but that's a Henry she's got in her hand." He watched Charley and the woman drag the body across the wide yard and to the side of the barn where they flopped it down. "That's the man riding the horse with the broken shoe, Pappy. So, the gang is just Charley and Gamble now. And that woman, whoever she is. It's also the answer to how many are there."

"You're right, Corcoran. If there were people holed up when Charley arrived I'm sure they would be part of whatever is going on down there. It is interesting hearing one shot and seeing two dead ones being brought out.

"Looks like they're gonna bury 'em right there." Pappy continued. "This would be a good time to ride 'em down. Come in at a hard gallop, guns on fire, boy."

"It would be," Corcoran said. He ducked back behind a large outcropping, stood up and stretched, looking around for a way to make it off the hill and to the burial party before the gang could turn and hide behind something and shoot back. "Company coming, Pappy," he said. He ducked back down and back to where he was. "Look toward the trail," he said and pointed at dust on the main road leading to the ranch. "Looks to be about three, maybe five miles out. They can only be coming here on that road."

"Let's get back to the horses and ride into that stand of trees down there. We'll be out of sight and much closer to the ranch." Pappy and Corcoran scrambled down off the ridge and mounted up. It was a hard and fast ride out from behind that rocky ridge, around toward the trail, and into a heavily forested area. They rode through stands of piñon and cedar and were near the incoming trail in short order. "It looks like we beat 'em, Pappy."

They tied off their horses and made their way to a stand of scrub cedar in time to see Wells town marshal Dean Whitaker ride right onto the ranch and wave a big hello to Humboldt Charley.

"Didn't expect this," Corcoran whispered.

Whitaker had his deputy with him, the snarly old Wallace Chandler, and they reined up where Charley and Gamble were digging the graves. "That's Chandler riding with Whitaker," Corcoran said. "They're being welcomed to the party, Pappy."

"It looks to me like Charley and Gamble were expecting them. You said the word was that Whitaker was on the take, I surely do believe you now. I'm more than curious about what that shooing was all about."

"After what those bastards did to Jeanne Moss, Pappy," and Corcoran took a long pause and deep breath. "With a very dead young girl and very dead outlaw. Well, that feller probably got out of line even by Charley's standards. She must have gotten in the way."

"They gotta die, every last one of 'em's gotta die, Corcoran." They were on their bellies sneaking through the timber trying to get as close to the action as possible. "We need to be a lot closer."

"We're gonna have to be satisfied with watching, old man. Can't go storming in, don't want to be spotted." Corcoran just smiled, scrunching down into the leaves. "Let's just watch the action."

"Have a little trouble, did you?" Marshal Whitaker said, almost a sneer in his voice. "He the man killed my deputy?" Whitaker was fully aware that Charley had done the killing of the deputy.

"What do you want, Whitaker?" Charley asked dropping the shovel and letting his hand hover near his sidearm. "Is it more gold? Or is this just a friendly welcome home visit?"

"You gonna make me welcome, Charley?" the fat marshal asked. It was an accepted fact in the west that you didn't dismount until asked to. Charley just waved his hand a bit, no smile or even a nod given.

Whitaker fought his way off his horse and limped over toward Charley and Gamble. Maria stood off to the side, that big Henry ready for action. "I thought we had a deal, Charley? Part of that deal was that you wouldn't cause any trouble in Wells. Killing one of my deputies is causing trouble, Charley. Want to explain?"

"Man was scum, Whitaker and you know it," Charley snarled, that big hand ready to pull on the fat marshal at the slightest wrong move. "He drew on me and you know that, too. What's the matter, we're not paying you enough? You looking to build that reputation?

"If that's it, fat man, make your play now." His eyes were slits, he was tensed and coiled and primed, and Whitaker kept his arms well out to the side, far away from his weapon.

"No, Charley, your payments have been fine, I'm not here to trouble you any. I just wanted to let you know that you did cause trouble in town, the town is somewhat riled, and it would be best if you stayed out of town for a while." He was shaking, fearful of Charley's temper and almost whining. "Please don't cause more trouble in town."

"Fat old coward," Charley laughed, turned away from Whitaker and took one step, whirled back, his iron out and cocked. Whitaker did not respond by going for his gun, instead he stood rock still and wet his pants. Charley uncocked the big Colt and shoved it back in the holster, laughing like the mad man he was. "Hey, look Maria. See the big man pee his pants?"

Charley pointed a finger at Whitaker. "Gotcha." He laughed all the way back to the ranch house, prodding Whitaker with every step. "I counted out a little bag of gold for you, marshal. Maybe you can buy some cajones instead of more food," and he stepped into the kitchen. Maria followed close behind with that Henry, not trusting Whitaker or Humboldt Charley for half a second.

Chandler never dismounted, never let go of the reins. Buford Gamble had a pick in one hand and his other was close to his side arm. "Keep yourself still old man," Gamble said. "This is between Charley and the marshal. Ain't got nothin' to do with you."

Gamble dropped the pick and started toward the ranch house. "Step off the horse and come on in out of the sun."

"What about those bodies. Aren't you gonna finish burying them? They'll get ripe fast out here."

"Want 'em buried? Grab a shovel," Gamble said walking through the kitchen door, chuckling a bit. Chandler scowled, stepped off his pony and followed Gamble into the kitchen, still smelling of burned powder and warm blood.

"That little scene pretty much changes things, Pappy," Corcoran said, sitting in the dirt with his back to a pine tree. "The Wells town marshal is working for Humboldt Charley and we're supposed to be here to arrest Humboldt Charley." A crooked smile was the best he could come up with. "What the hell do we do now?"

Pappy shook his head, scowling in the direction of the ranch house, making marks in the dirt with a twig. "Can't say I've ever been in this position, Corcoran. We don't have any authority out here at all. None," he emphasized. "Our authority ended at the Eureka County line and you were depending on Whitaker to honor that authority. We can't arrest anyone on this ranch, we can't kill anyone in that building. We're in a mess," he said, getting to his feet.

They moved quickly back to their horses and mounted up. The ride back to their camp was slow and filled with conversation. "Maybe a cup of strong coffee will help some," Corcoran chuckled. "Only thing we can do is pack up and ride to Elko, Pappy. This is Elko County, so the county sheriff has to be the ultimate law. You got a better idea?"

"Not a one," Pappy Somerset laughed. "Not a one." It was an easy ride through the trees and over a slight humpback before dropping down to their camp. The fire was kindled, and the coffee pot prepared.

"If we hurry it's at least a two-day ride to Elko and only the railroad town of Halleck between here and there. Let's have a nice hot meal, pack it up and ride, Pappy."

"We can't even stop in Wells to send a wire to the sheriff,"

Corcoran said adding more wood to the fire. "Whitaker surely has eyes and ears all over that town. We'd best not be seen in Halleck either. Elko might be a huge county, but you can bet Whitaker would know where we were going and why, and I mean immediately." He dropped down on his haunches, messed with the fire, wondering how it was a man could carry a badge and work hand in hand with a murderous bunch like Humboldt Charley's gang.

"We'll skirt wide of that town, across near the old Humboldt Wells, and pick up the emigrant road in. The only thing that would make this worse is if Humboldt Charley was holding a hostage."

"You don't suppose that's what that young girl was, do you?" Pappy Somerset's jaw was so tight it was a miracle the bones and teeth didn't explode. "They didn't seem to have much trouble taking Jeanne Moss and then just leaving her to die. Do you think that girl was being held?"

"That's a question that will be asked when we take those bastards down, Pappy. We'll ask that question just before we kill 'em dead. I want to kill those men twice each." The anger and frustration was taken out on the fire as Corcoran stirred it enough to send sparks high into the cold fall day.

"His name is Billy Kick and he's been sheriff in Elko for a hunnert years, Pappy. He's a tough old bird but as honest a man as I've known. Don't pay no attention to some of the things he might say about me when we walk in, now," Corcoran said, joshing Pappy Somerset some.

The ride into Elko followed along the Humboldt River and the railroad, skirted Halleck and the north end of the Ruby Mountains, and settled in the broad plain that hosted Elko. Since the time of California's gold rush, thousands of immigrants had traveled on the road. Wagon wheels had left deep ruts in the ground. It was many years, basically after the railroad, before grass was able to grow back, so many horses, mules, and oxen had grazed the trail.

They encountered little traffic and there were no storms, so the two days went by quickly. Elko was a railroad town with the tracks right through the middle of downtown. There were commercial districts on both sides of the tracks and the depot was almost a gathering and social place for residents.

Ranches had grown up around the area, some large and prosperous. Corcoran and Somerset checked their horses and the mule at a livery and found rooms at the Commercial Hotel, which overlooked the tracks. They took rooms facing the street, not the tracks. Still covered in trail dust, the two men sauntered down Commercial Street toward the court-house and the sheriff's office.

Elko was a busy town surrounded by large ranches, an active commercial district served the ranches, railroad, immigrants, and a large local native population. Corcoran and Somerset passed ladies in their finery and buckaroos in town to whoop it up a bit. They saw grease stained railroad workers, Indians looking for handouts, and business men sweeping the board walkways.

"I think you'll like Billy Kick. You're probably about the same age. He left the army after the war and came west. He's well educated, coming out of the military academy, and will fight at the drop of a pennyweight offer."

"I think I like him already," Pappy answered, "Think he'll even believe what we have to tell him."

The sheriff had his offices and jail in a building attached to the Elko County Courthouse with access to the main building. It was a short walk from the hotel and it was getting late in the day when Corcoran and Somerset made their way into Kick's office.

"Somebody get the brass band out and playing," Billy Kick

said, jumping to his feet and gathering Terrence Corcoran in a bear hug. "The wild Irishman has come to save the world?" he asked, "Or create more havoc and pain? Which is it, Corcoran?"

Corcoran ignored the comment, but with a smile playing across his broad face introduced Pappy. "Bill, I want you to meet Pappy Somerset and then we need to take you to a friendly saloon and ruin your day."

"I was afraid of that, Terrence," Kick said. "Pappy Somerset. Black Hills? Powder River?"

"I was hoping you were the same Billy Kick when Corcoran told me you were the sheriff. It's been some time, Bill. You were a cavalry major then and a fine officer," he said, shaking the sheriff's hand. "Some place we can hike off to? We got a hell of yarn to tell."

CHAPTER 14

"I GOT THE WIRE FROM SEAGRAM IN EUREKA, CORCORAN, about the Eureka bank and the dead posse, and the information on the Belmont dust-up, but your name wasn't included. Whitaker's been a pain in my side for years, but what you're telling me goes way past a pain." Sheriff Billy Kick was in his fifties, two hundred fifty pounds of solid big man, and his steel-blue eyes were a cold flint as he listened to Corcoran's story.

"Humboldt Charley has eyes and ears all over this corner of Nevada, but knowing where he is gives me a couple of ideas, Corcoran. Did you tell Whitaker you were trailing Charley?"

"Sure, did and he told me I had no jurisdiction and get the hell out. We got on Charley's trail the next morning. While we were out looking for his winter home, Charley rode into town and killed one of Whitaker's deputies, and I reminded that fat bastard that I had warned him. It's a mess, Bill."

The three were sitting at a table at the back of the Round-up Saloon on Commercial, mugs of cold beer making rings on the table. This was a cowboy saloon and catered to the cattlemen and buckaroos of the area. Poker and faro were the table games of choice, some attractive working girls were available for the proper incentive, and the cigars were two-bits, shipped straight from Virginia and the best on the market.

"If I put a posse together the word would spread faster than if I sent a wire," Kick chuckled. "However, if the two of you and me and a deputy were to ride out to check on a cattle rustling, never mentioning Humboldt Charley, we might pull it off.

"I know that ranch and the lady you described. She's Maria Lopez, used to run a high-class house in Denver called Consuela's. She came here from Denver, and is well known as a blackmailer, schemer, and killer. She's wanted for robbing banks in Denver and probably Salt Lake City as well. I've sent wires to Whitaker more than once to arrest her."

"Why didn't he?" Pappy Somerset asked.

"Said my information was wrong. No such woman in the area. I've never seen the ranch, only heard about it, and what you describe is what I heard. They call her Maria, and Charley pays her and Whitaker protection money. With your help, Corcoran, we can take out Charley, Maria, and Whitaker in one little ride.

"You boys get a good supper, sleep in a good bed, and be ready to ride about five tomorrow morning. I'll meet you at the livery and we'll make sure the stable hand knows we're investigating some cattle thefts."

The sheriff drained his beer mug and left the saloon, nodding to a few of the buckaroos as he walked out. "He's got fire in those eyes, Terrence. Whitaker ain't gonna live through this."

"Neither is Charley," Corcoran said. "Law dogs are funny fellers, Pappy. When one goes bad it casts a shadow on all the rest of us. Whitaker needs to be gone. I want to send a wire to Seagram letting him know we're in Elko, but not why.

Then we'll see if we can find a couple of sides of beef for supper. You're a fine man, Pappy Somerset, but I need someone else's cooking tonight."

It took another round of cold beer before they were able to make their way to the telegraph office, then to the fine dining room at the hotel and steaks followed by fresh apple pie. "Do you realize, Terrence, this is the first place the two of us has walked into that some charming young lady didn't fling herself at you?" Corcoran chuckled.

"There's a little place around the corner I want to visit before I hit the hotel," Corcoran said. "You're welcome to join me, Pappy."

"No, Terrence, I'm gonna put these old bones between the covers, I think. I'll see you in the morning." He smiled as he headed for his rooms and a warm night in a soft bed. *I swear that man knows everybody in this old state.*

Corcoran walked into the Silver Lady Saloon and Dance Hall and nodded to the big man standing near the faro table. "Evening, Jimmy," he said to the security man. He made his way through heavy traffic to the bar.

"Nice to see you again, Slim," he said to the barman. "How about a hot coffee laced with some fine brandy?"

"I won't stand for any trouble, Corcoran," Slim Bayard said in a growl.

"I'm not a trouble makin' man, Slim, but it wouldn't hurt my feelings if you found it in your warm and friendly heart to pay me back that fifty I fronted you. Doesn't appear your effort paid off much."

"I'll give you a piece of it, Corcoran. That's all I can do." Bayard's attitude changed some. He poured about a third of a cup of coffee in a deep mug and filled it to the top with under the bar brandy. That good stuff. "Those boys was rotten thieves, Corcoran. Took me for every dime. Never had no mind to open a saloon or give me my own table."

"I think I mentioned that a time or two, Slim. Give me what you can. I felt bad when you just up and runned off. Made me feel like I didn't really know you." Corcoran never took the smile off his Irish mug and Slim's whole attitude deflated measurably, his shoulders drooping, his chin tucked in, and his eyes averted.

"I'm sorry about that, too, Corcoran. Here's twenty. It's the best I can do right now," and he slipped a gold double eagle onto the oak bar. "Are you going to be in town long?"

"Maybe," is all Corcoran said, and he sipped his brandy, tucking the gold coin in his pants pocket. "You able to take care of those hoot-owls? They had to be after others with short pockets and no brains."

"Last I heard they were headed toward Denver It ain't that I can't think, Corcoran," Slim said, getting a little of his growl back, "but that deal sounded so sweet. They would open the saloon and I would have my own tables, run the gambling end of the partnership."

"I think the old saying goes something like, if it sounds too good to be true, it's not. I think I even mentioned that a time or two. Save up some more gold, Slim. I'll be making more than just this visit."

It was several cups of coffee later that he ambled into the hotel, a smile on his face and warmth in his belly. *Tonight, a little piece of old Slim, but tomorrow, I'm taking the biggest piece out of Humboldt Charley's soul. Charley and Whitaker will die, or I'll know the reason why.*

Belmont Town Marshal Mason Tetford was doing his best to get about on crutches, his leg in a cast from foot to groin. He had Tim Kleinfelt bring a peach crate from the banker. "He sure don't need them," he joshed when Kleinfelt brought it into the office. It was early morning and Tetford sat in his chair, that leg stretched straight out, resting on the wooden crate. He was talking with his first visitor of the day.

"I can't force you not to do this, Jeanne, but I can ask you not to. Besides the obvious danger, what would be the purpose? Some kind of revenge?"

"Not revenge in the true sense of the word, marshal, but very close." Jeanne Moss frowned. She rode into Belmont that morning to see her brother Jeremy, still under Doc Patterson's care. His wound was infected and there were fears for the boy's leg. Jeremy was going to be in Belmont for some time.

"I know you think I'm just a young girl," she said to Marshal Tetford, "helpless and dumb as cold honey, but remember I've worked right alongside my father on that ranch from the day I could sit a horse. I'm a crack shot, I could whup your deputy in half a second, and I need to know the man who killed my father is gonna pay for it."

Everyone in that part of Nevada knew Bill Moss and his temper. Those that worked for him held him in the highest regard and feared that temper. That banker would challenge old Moss just so far and then back off. They also respected his work ethic and his honesty. Marshal Tetford could see Bill Moss writ deep in daughter Jeanne.

"I'm gonna see to it that Humboldt Charley will never attack another girl and do the things that he did to me. I'm not gonna kill him, Mason. I'm not a murderer, he is, but I'm gonna see to it that he's either dead or bound in chains. He will never touch another girl the way he did me," she said, her eyes blazing with hatred.

She had her little fists held tight, the knuckles white and straining under the pressure. Her face was set in a frown the likes of which Tetford had never seen.

Tetford laughed right out loud at the comment about Kleinfelt and knew that what Jeanne Moss was saying was the truth. "But riding off to Eureka and then chasing after Pappy and Corcoran," and he paused, shaking his head. "Your brother's as stove up as I am and can't ride with you, Jeanne. Who would you take? Surely you're not thinking of riding off alone."

"I was," she said, a smile spreading across her face. "Pa and me have rode that trail many times, Mason. I've got a good handgun and my rifle. I'll pack a mule, and I'll stay near but not at the stage stops at night. If my ankle hadn't been so bad I would have ridden off with Pappy and Terrence that day." She got to her feet and paced around the little office, stopping near the potbelly stove.

"I'm sixteen, Mason. I've lost my ma and pa, my brother might lose his leg, I've been brutally attacked. I must do this, make this ride and see justice done, for me, for the ranch, for the family. Those men are going to pay for what they did, and I'm going to be there when they do." Her entire demeanor told the marshal to back off. She had her hands on her hips, her mouth was set and not a smile in sight. If eyes could talk, hers said, "no argument."

"Like I said, I can't stop you, but I wish you wouldn't do this." He knew his words meant nothing and his big regret was that he wasn't going with her. Tetford and her father talked about Jeanne and Jeremy often, and the marshal was aware that Jeanne Moss was tougher than her older brother. "I wish I was going with you, Jeanne. You've been through hell, don't ruin the rest of your life."

"That ain't the plan, Mason," she said, a devastatingly beautiful smile lighting her face. He may not have said yes to her plan, but it sounded like he just gave his blessing. "Get yourself well. I'll be back, and the Moss family ranch will survive." As young as she was, Tetford knew deep down that she would find Pappy, help in the capture or killing of Humboldt Charley, and return to ramrod that huge ranch.

She gave him a hug and a little peck on the cheek and walked out of the office. Tetford noticed that she wasn't even limping on her twisted ankle. *It's gonna take one hell of a man to rope and tie that one,* he chuckled. *No girl should ever have to go through what she did, and as a betting man, my odds are in favor of her being the one to kill Humboldt Charley.*

From Belmont back to the Moss ranch was taken at a fast trot, slow walk, fast trot and the thirty miles were eaten up by Jeanne's young ranch gelding. She had trained that pony from the day he was foaled, four years ago. She lit out the next morning, a mule packed for the hundred-mile ride, telling the ranch foreman that she would be back as soon as possible and to operate as if she or her father were there.

Trailing a pack mule meant a much slower trip and Jeanne was able to enjoy the early fall weather and sights on the ride. Thunderstorms could pop up quickly, and an early morning frost would not be out of line. Jeanne Moss had ridden with the buckaroos for several years, thought like them, acted like them. A one-hundred-mile ride? No buckaroo ever wants to get out of the saddle.

Riding a great circle on a summer grazing area would put a cowboy in the saddle from sunup or before to sundown or after. She felt far better in the saddle than she ever did out of it. She planned a big meal at early morning and late evening, with whatever she shoved in a pocket to take care of mid-day hunger. The purpose of the ride was to end the life of Humboldt Charley, but that didn't mean she couldn't enjoy every minute of riding through the beauty of the high mountain desert called Nevada.

She was prepared for foul weather and long hours in the saddle. Once she connected with the main road from Austin to Eureka, she often had the company of fellow travelers, and never encountered the least difficulty. When the hog-leg tied to her didn't catch their eyes, the Henry rifle in the saddle leather did. She found, on arrival, that Eureka County Sheriff Fred Seagram was expecting her.

"Glad you made it safe, Miss Moss. Marshal Tetford wired to expect you. You made quite an impression on Terrence Corcoran as well. Sit down, please, and let's have a little chat." She brightened noticeably at the Corcoran comment.

From the moment he'd found her hiding in those rocks high in the mountains, she'd had good thoughts about the man. He was tender but strong, decisive but open to suggestion, and his eyes spoke the truth just as his smile warmed the heart. *Sissy little girl stuff,* she told herself often, when he crept into her thoughts. The thought also always brought a smile.

"If your idea of a chat is to talk me out of chasing down the vile men who attacked me, killed my father, and hurt my brother, you can save your breath. I only want you to tell me where you think Pappy Somerset and Terrence Corcoran are right now."

"I know what those men did, Miss Moss. I can't imagine your pain and suffering, and I'm terribly sorry for your father's death, so you must reconsider what you're contemplating. Corcoran's a good lawman, he's deadly in a gunfight, and he's traveling with one of the best trackers in the west. They'll catch up with Humboldt Charley and his gang and justice will be done.

"Your father has deep roots in Eureka County, as you well know, and was a good friend. I'll miss him. I've watched you grow into the lovely young lady you are and don't doubt for a minute that you can do what you're planning. We just need to talk about the situation."

She was filled with hatred and didn't understand what Seagram was saying, didn't hear that he was supporting what she planned. "I will be there to see those men dead or in chains, Sheriff Seagram, with or without your help. This man Terrence Corcoran saved my life, nursed me, fed me, and saved me after those men attacked me. I want to stand next to that man when he hands out this justice you mentioned."

Seagram shook his head, scowled at the beautiful young girl and debated whether to tell her where Somerset and Corcoran were. She stood near the potbelly stove, hands on hips, almost glaring at the sheriff. "You've got more spunk than most men I know, Jeanne Moss." He couldn't hold his smile, wanted to put his arms around the girl and knew he couldn't. He knew he was going to help her, though.

"Let's you and me take a little walk. There's an old man I want you to meet. I hope you're hungry." She nodded, gave him a bit of a crooked smile, and followed the big man out the door and onto the main street. He led her across the street to a large, ornate building, fitted out with Victorian charm. "Gingerbread," she exclaimed, pointing at all the elegant woodwork. The sign across the second story balcony read, Jackson House. The building was bright red with white trim, and was the centerpiece of the town, even overshadowing the Eureka Opera House.

"The only building this big in Belmont is the courthouse," Jeanne said as they walked into the dining room. Seagram led them to a large table that would seat at least six people and held a chair for her.

He nodded to a man in a white shirt and string tie, with a red apron tucked in around his waist. "Good day, Mr. Jackson. Miss Moss and I would like the luncheon special and would you see if Sandy McAuliffe is in the saloon and ask him to join us for dinner, please?"

"Yes, sir, Sheriff Seagram. Out special is pork chops, mashed potatoes, fresh corn, and Miss Marian's sourdough biscuits. I'll find Mac right away." Jackson was from New York originally, and his family had been in the hotel and restaurant business for several generations. The Jackson

House in Eureka was a little brother to a larger, more elegant Jackson House in the big city in the east.

"Old Mac, like Pappy Somerset was an army scout, Miss Moss, and if you promise him beans and biscuits at least once a day, and side meat and hard tack once a day, he'll lead you right to Corcoran." He was chuckling, but she saw hard truth in his eyes.

Jeanne giggled at the way Seagram said that and remembered how Pappy Somerset used to come to the ranch to visit and always asked for beans and biscuits. It must be an army thing, she mused. "Please, call me Jeanne, Sheriff Seagram. Will it be safe for me to ride with him?" All at once the fear set in, blood red visions of what happened on Flat Top Ridge. All the terror returned, the men and their foul smells, the pain and humiliation.

She was almost shaking, the tears were just moments away, when Sandy McAuliffe plopped himself down at the table, a mug of cold beer in hand. "Miss. Sheriff." He nodded with a smile in her direction, and a questioning in Seagram's.

She saw an older man with white, nicely attended whiskers that hung down to the middle of his chest and a full head of long white hair in a braid that stretched down his back. He had a smashed up black hat in his hand and she could see two scars that spread across his open, friendly face. That he was a fighting man at least at one time was evident. She understood too, that he had good manners.

He was dressed in well-worn buckskins, his moccasins reached almost to his knees, and were tied with rough-cut rawhide laces. He wore a massive knife at his side. She was taken by the handle. It was an intricately carved ivory handle that was obviously well-worn. She could remember many knives with horn or wooden handles, but never anything like this her first thought was *I want one just like it.*

He saw the interest in his knife and pulled it from its

pouch. "The handle's from a walrus, miss. You know what a walrus is?"

"I've seen drawings, Mr. McAuliffe. That knife's beautiful."

"Shot the walrus myself, I did," he said. "I was supposed to be lookin' fer gold up there in Alaska, but they be too many side things to see and do. Never found any gold," he chuckled. "Made the knife at my own fire and anvil." He smiled with his entire face as he tucked the knife away. "Ever been to Alaska, girl?" She shook her head in amazement at the man and the way he talked.

His eyes, gray and bright, danced with good humor, and his face, crinkled and wrinkled, spoke of strength as well as humor. She did her best not to stare, but those scars spoke to a life of violence, and her fears, returned. *I want to trust this man. His eyes tell me I can, but what if I'm wrong.*

"Sandy McAuliffe, meet Jeanne Moss," Seagram said. "Sandy's cousin rode with the posse that Humboldt Charley's gang killed after robbing the bank here," he said to Jeanne. "Jeanne's father was killed, and Charley's gang abducted her and held her for two horrible days, Sandy."

"I know you remember Terrence Corcoran, and I'm sure you've dealt with Pappy Somerset." McAuliffe's eyes saddened when Seagram told about Jeanne's ordeal and brightened some at the mention of Somerset.

"Pappy and I rode for the same army outfit years ago, Fred. And sure, I remember the crazy Irishman. Corcoran and I have had our tussles, but he's as honest a man as there is. You're leading me somewhere, Fred Seagram. Spell it out."

It was a long lunch as Fred Seagram told the story, Jeanne adding things the sheriff wasn't aware of, and McAuliffe asking questions along the way. The pork chops and mashed potatoes were long gone, apple pie was eaten, and Seagram needed to get back to the office.

"Let's you and me, take a stroll, little lady," Sandy McAuliffe said. "I think better when I'm outside in the clean air. Besides, I like a little nip after a meal like that." He held her chair, helped her into a winter coat, and they walked out of the café and into a fall wind blowing leaves and dust around Eureka.

"Me hovel is just up the street, miss," he laughed. "Let's bring your horse and mule and talk about what it is we have to do. It's a terrible thing you've been through and I'm not sure revenge will bring you the peace of mind you're looking for, but it might help a bit. I've got a touch of revenge in my own heart right now."

They walked the two blocks up the hill, south of the main street to a plot of ground, well-tended, that featured a small log and clapboard cabin, small barn, and three corrals, two of which stood empty. Sandy helped her unload the mule and unsaddle her gelding, and they put them in the empty corrals.

"It's always best if you have some idea where you're going and who you'll be fightin' before you engage," Sandy said, ushering her into his cabin. It was essentially one room with a bed on one side, a table and two chairs in the middle, and a cook stove on the other side. "I call it Castle McAuliffe," he joshed, stoking the fire in the stove and putting on a fresh pot of coffee. He rummaged around a bit and came up with a flask as well. "Don't mind if I do," he chuckled, tagging a long swig of good whiskey.

It was the first time she found herself alone with a man she didn't know, except for the time with Corcoran, and she looked about, almost feeling trapped. Could she make it to the door if he attacked? Could she fight him off? Would he use that knife? And then she saw the face, his smile and soft eyes, not the scars. She heard his voice, and remembered how Corcoran had talked to her, how her fears slowly ebbed.

I hope I'm right. I'm going to listen to what he says and then make up my mind, but right now, I feel I can trust this old mountain man.

"It's best that we travel light," he said. He poured them each a cup of boiling coffee, left enough room in his cup for a healthy dose of whiskey, lit a pipe that smelled heavenly to Jeanne, and continued. "We'll leave the mule here and ride fast. As Seagram said, the last word he got was Corcoran and Somerset were in Elko. There's a trail north from here, through Skelton, and into Elko. We can be there in two days."

Jeanne settled into her chair, across the table from Sandy McAuliffe, and looked deep into those lively eyes and made up her mind. "Any man that attempts to touch me, ever again, will die, Mr. McAuliffe."

"After what you and Fred told me, I'll help you kill 'em. I'll not harm a hair on your pretty head, girl, and I'll kill any man that tries."

She surprised this lively but hard-bitten man when she stuck her hand out, as a man would, and they shook hands, a partnership formed.

CHAPTER 15

Corcoran was at the livery before five setting the pack on his mule when Billy Kick walked in. "Mornin' Terrence. Meet George Anders."

"Good to meet you, Anders. Riding with this wild man must be a chore." Corcoran shook the man's hand and gave him a good looking over. Anders was probably around thirty or so, about five eight and close to two hundred pounds of solid muscle. He wore a Colt Peacemaker in a cross-draw holster and Corcoran saw a handmade knife with bone handle stuck in the deputy's boot.

Anders wore canvas trousers held up with heavy leather suspenders, a red wool shirt over long johns, and a rough buckskin jacket. Corcoran couldn't take his eyes off that jacket. It featured numerous stains, some of which may have been blood, some obviously whiskey, and others that Corcoran felt he wouldn't ask about. "Nice coat," he said.

"Yup. Big elk it was. I shot it, ate it, and now I'm wearing its skin." He laughed at his own joke, his eyes dancing with humor. "Think we'll find that mad man?"

"Humboldt Charley's hours are numbered," Pappy

Somerset said, leading his horse out of the barn. "It's two days to Maria's ranch, and two days to Charley's end."

"I told the boys in the office that we would be heading for Skelton to investigate some cattle thefts, so hopefully, Charley won't know what's hit him when we get there." Billy Kick was mounted on a tall gelding that looked like it could outrun any blue norther that challenged it. "Let's get moving, boys."

They rode out of Elko on the main road east, following the intercontinental railroad. "Feels like we got us a storm brewing, Terrence." Pappy Somerset was watching heavy clouds coming across the vast Nevada plain. "Wind, Terrence, that's what we'll have. Wind and more wind, and then some rain, and early morning wet snow."

"Is he always so full of cheer and good news?" Kick chuckled. "But I think he's right."

The ride to Wells was long and slow. Commercial wagons moving on the well-used road slowed their progress. As they rode dust from cattle herds still being brought in from summer range could be seen along the sides of the Ruby Mountains, and the peaks of those mountains, some well over ten thousand feet, always to their south east carried traces of early snow.

"We'll make Halleck about sunset, but we'll need to camp well outside that town," Kick said.

"I thought the name was Camp Halleck," Pappy said.

"It was. The army moved. It's filled with railroad people and still many soldiers from nearby Fort Halleck, but you can bet good money that Humboldt Charley will have friends in that town. When was the last time you were there, George?"

"When I brought Shoshone Mike in, Bill. I make that about six months ago. Harry Jensen is the town marshal and he's not someone we want to see us. I'm sure he's as dirty as

Whitaker and Charley would get the word about us immediately."

"What's with the town marshals being so crooked, Kick? You're the sheriff, can't you straighten things out?" Corcoran knew Billy Kick from years ago and always knew him to be a good lawman. The idea of town marshals in his jurisdiction acting like outlaws concerned him.

"For the most part they're elected just like me, Corcoran. They gotta get caught breaking the law before I can do anything. With elected town marshals in most of the little communities, it would be foolish for me to put a deputy in each one, too. The marshals have working agreements with some of these outlaw gangs and are well protected. In return, the gangs leave those towns alone."

"Sounds like a sweet deal for the marshals and the outlaws," Corcoran snarled. "I don't know how you can tolerate it, though. Maybe we can rough up this Harry Jenkins on the way back with Humboldt Charley's body." Billy Kick chuckled, nodded his head, and pulled his heavy coat a little tighter.

Just as Pappy Somerset predicted the wind came at gale force blowing leaves, grasses, and dirt in every direction all at the same time. There was cold air in that wind and everyone knew they would find snow on the ground in the morning.

They found campsite some five miles east of Halleck, well off the main road and set up for the night. They were in a stand of mixed aspen and cottonwood, fresh water from the beginnings of the Humboldt River, with plenty of grass available for the animals.

"We'll make Humboldt Wells late tomorrow, and be at the ranch early the following day," Pappy Somerset said, stoking the fire with some dried cottonwood. "But we'll be riding in a storm, boys, count on it."

He wasn't wrong. The group fought strong wind and icy rain when they had their coffee and sourdough biscuits the next morning. In place of sidemeat they softened some good venison jerky in the hot coffee. It was the first good storm of the fall and would slow the group considerably. At mid-day, Corcoran rode up next to Kick.

"We'll not make Humboldt Wells today, Bill."

"You're right, Corcoran. Got any ideas? We need to be really close to that ranch and set up a solid camp to work from. The Humboldt Wells would have been very good."

The Humboldt River begins at Humboldt Wells. A community grew up near the springs, but with the railroad and emigrant trail off a bit, the community moved, and the town of Wells was created at the railroad and the main east-west road. A road south led eventually to Pioche and extended north into Idaho. There were some that called the area four corners, but the town's name was Wells.

"We'll have snow on the ground come morning, Bill," Corcoran said. "We're simply going to have to extend our plan by one day. We'll get close to the Humboldt Wells later today, then move as close to that ranch as possible tomorrow and set up for our ambush."

"I guess you're right, Corcoran. I just hate to get slowed down like this."

"I'll have a chat with the big boy and get this storm done with for you, Bill," Corcoran laughed, lightly punching the sheriff in the shoulder. "Pappy' ll have us another good camp site. We were through here just a couple of days ago, remember. He's a gem when it comes to reading the landscape."

"I don't understand, McAuliffe. Are you looking for Sheriff Kick or Humboldt Charley?" Ken Wilder was standing near the gate to his blacksmith shop in Skelton, at the base of the Ruby Mountains giving McAuliffe and Jeanne Moss a good look. "You'll probably find Billy Kick in Elko, but if you're chasing after Charley, you'd be better off heading for Wells.

"Word around these parts is that outlaws are safe in the Wells area." He laughed as he said that. "You're an old man, McAuliffe riding with a young girl and looking for the likes of Humboldt Charley? You're a bigger fool than I thought."

Sandy McAuliffe and Jeanne Moss rode into Skelton early their second morning having camped just south of the town. McAuliffe had had dealings with Ken Wilder in the past and hoped he might get some information on Humboldt Charley and his gang of outlaws.

"Nice to know that, Ken." Sandy McAuliffe had a nasty scowl on his face as he turned his horse back onto the road through the little town nestled at the western flank of those high mountains. "Guess we'll head for Elko."

He and Jeanne rode north, and she asked why Elko if Charley might be in Wells. "Said that for Ken's sake," he chuckled. "Mr. Wilder was a highwayman once, spent some time in the Carson City Prison, and may have contacts with Charley. Don't worry your head about it, we're going to Wells. It looks like we'll be riding straight into a storm, though."

They followed along the base of the Ruby Mountains all the rest of the day, fighting winds that grew stronger as the hours passed by. Rain began to fall as they eventually connected with the emigrant road and turned east. "Let's ride for at least another hour, Jeanne, if you're up to it, and then make camp. This looks to be a strong storm for this early in the season."

"I'm fine Sandy. Chousing calves in the high mountains all day makes a ride like today almost a holiday." She almost giggled when he scowled at her. "Do you have some kind of plan?"

"I think so. We'll discuss that when we're settled in camp.

Glad you insisted on bringing that canvas from your mule. We'll need it for a lean-to with this wind and rain."

"I've been to Elko with pa a couple of times, Sandy, but I've never been east. Where are we right now?"

"You're lucky I've got my humor under control, little lady, because what I want to say is, 'damned if I know'." They both had a good laugh at that. "Actually, we're just a few miles from a little town called Halleck. Used be called Camp Halleck and was an army camp. The army moved south, and the camp became a community. Kind of a rough and tumble little place. No town for a lady."

They found a nice stand of trees off the road and set up camp. Sandy hobbled the horses in good grass and looked for some dry wood for the fire. Jeanne laid out their bedrolls under the canvas and worked with Sandy to get the fire going. "Someone was here last night, Sandy. This fire pit was used recently. Think they'll be back?"

"Let's hope not," he chuckled, bringing another armload of cottonwood to the fire.

Supper was sidemeat and coffee and breakfast was coffee with some jerky floating in it, and a cold biscuit or two. "It's gonna be a miserable ride, Jeanne, and I'm not sure we'll make it all the way to Humboldt Wells. If it gets a little bit colder, the mud might stiffen up some, and that would help."

"If we spend tonight at Humboldt Wells, then what? How will we find Terrence and Pappy?"

"Only way I know is to ride into the town of Wells and ask about them. We don't want to mention Humboldt Charley. Remember what Ken Wilder said," They were wearing all their extra clothing, had winter coats buckled up tight, and were wearing rain slickers as well as they paced their horses all day long. They rode for long periods at a fast trot and then slowed to a walk, letting their horses catch their breath, and then back into a trot.

Jeanne's young gelding rarely breathed hard, but they did have to slow for McAuliffe's horse. "You're riding a ranch horse that's used to working all day and I'm riding a horse like me. Old and tired," McAuliffe chuckled. "Even so, we might make Humboldt Springs tonight. This snow has made the trail an easy ride. It's the wind that I hate."

The snow had made the mud thicker and easier to ride through. "It's the heavy snow with a crust of ice on top that ruins good horses," McAuliffe said. "Ice cuts their legs and will cripple one up fast."

"My dad always tied rags around their feet when we had to ride through snow like that. We won't have that problem with this storm, though," she said.

The wind, rain, and heavy snow eased off late in the afternoon and Sandy McAuliffe was able to see the surrounding countryside. "We'll get off the road and onto the Humboldt Wells trail just ahead, Jeanne. How are you holding up?"

"I'm cold, Sandy, my ankle hurts, and I'm hungry," she laughed. "Other than that, it's been just a wonderful day. How about you?"

"My ankle's fine," is all he said. He wanted his pipe and a hot fire, wanted a sip of good whiskey and a hot fire. Wanted a hot meal and a hot fire "It'll be mighty close to sunset when we reach the springs, but there's good water, good grass, and we'll get a fine fire blazing." They were hunkered down in the saddles, heads bowed to the wind, both thinking good thoughts about that fire and just how big they might make it.

CHAPTER 16

"WE LOST ONE DAY, IS ALL, BILL," CORCORAN SAID, WARMING his hands near a blazing fire. "We can ride right up near that ranch tomorrow, set a camp, scout out the situation and still have time to attack if things are right. Next time we'll work it out ahead of time so there won't be a storm." He had to chuckle watching Elko Sheriff Billy Kick fume and fuss over not being able to ride through the storm and attack Humboldt Charley.

Wild Bill Kick had to laugh as well, listening to Terrence Corcoran's joshing. He poured another cup of coffee, lacing it from his flask. "All these years, Corcoran, and I've never seen you riled. I'm cold, I'm wet, and I haven't whupped on anybody for two days. Humboldt Charley doesn't know what's coming at him." Kick stormed around the camp, kicking rocks and snow, putting even more wood on the already large fire. "I'm riled," he snarled and laughed at the same time.

"Yup, you are," Corcoran chuckled. "How long have you worked for this riled up old sheriff, Mr. Anders?"

"Some time now, Corcoran. You get used to it after a bit."

Kick just harrumphed some and stormed about. "He'll get tired soon and we can get on with supper."

It had been a grueling and frustrating day for the four men, fighting their way through snow blown about by severe wind and freezing cold. They left Humboldt Wells just after dawn for the ride to the ranch where they hoped Humboldt Charley and his gang were still holed up, but never got more than ten, maybe twelve miles out before turning back.

"We don't even know where we are, Kick," Corcoran finally said when they rode into a copse of trees to get out of the gale. "Even if we make it to the ranch we won't be able to do anything, anyway. Let's go back to the wells and wait out the storm."

Kick was the kind of man who thrived on action but was astute enough to understand what Corcoran was saying. He saw the same things in the faces of Pappy Somerset and his deputy, Anders. They turned back and as the day slowly came to an end, it was obvious the storm was abating.

"Don't know why that famous tracker of yours didn't at least shoot an antelope for our supper," Kick grumbled. Corcoran laughed at that and whacked Wild Bill Kick on the back.

"You haven't been paying attention, wild man. Pappy shot a deer an hour ago. We'll have fresh meat for supper tonight."

As he said that, Pappy Somerset rode up alongside the sheriff. "Well, looks like he spent most of the summer in someone's alfalfa field, Corcoran. This is one big meaty old muley for sure. Took me some time to get him cleaned and skinned with this old storm blowin' things around.

"Long as it stays cold like this, we'll be eatin' fresh venison for a week or more, sheriff." He didn't get any response from Billy Kick, and gave him a hard look. "What's this? You don't like fresh venison? Is he being grumpy, Corcoran?"

"Yup, but you can bet he'll eat his fair share."

"We got company coming," Pappy Somerset said, walking to his saddle and rig laid out near the fire. He pulled his rifle from its scabbard and moved back away from the fire. Corcoran and Kick had their revolvers in hand and stood back twenty feet or so from the fire. Anders pulled his weapon and scampered into the brush ducking into the snow behind some high sage.

It was a furious fire after the sheriff had stoked it several times. "Must be like a beacon in the middle of the desert," Corcoran chuckled, squatting under a heavy sage. "Probably see that all the way to Elko."

"Let 'em get close but don't shoot unless I do," Kick snarled, ducking down onto his knees in the brush. "Easy now," he said, quietly, as two riders came down the trail at a walk. One was husky but mostly hidden inside a heavy winter coat and wrapped in a wool blanket.

The second rider, considerably smaller, was equally wrapped against the storm. Both riders looked worn out and apparently were drawn in by the large fire that Bill Kick kept building. "Hello, the camp," The large man yelled. "We're friendly, mean no harm. Just want to get near your fire."

"Ride in then and make no fast moves," Bill Kick yelled back. "The fire's hot and so's the coffee, stranger."

Sandy McAuliffe and Jeanne Moss rode slowly into the camp and dismounted, simply ground tying their tired horses. McAuliffe unwrapped himself from his iced over wool blanket and folded it over the saddle, helping Jeanne get out of hers.

"Well, glory be, it's Jeanne Moss," Terrence Corcoran bellowed, taking three big steps across the camp and gathering the girl into his arms. "What on earth have we got here?" he said, looking into her gleaming eyes.

"Been lookin' for you, Terrence," she said. He walked her over to the fire, so she could spread her blanket and sit down.

"Been a long ride," she murmured taking the coffee offered by Corcoran.

George Anders took their horses and he and Pappy Somerset unsaddled them and tied them to the long line with their horses. It didn't take long for them to kick some snow aside and get into the good grass. "You know them, Pappy?" Anders asked. "That's a mighty pretty, young lady."

"She is at that, young man," Pappy chuckled. "And she's the reason we're on this hunt of ours. That's Jeanne Moss, the girl Humboldt Charley's gang abducted and held for two days. The only reason she's alive is because of Terrence Corcoran."

"I'd ride a thousand miles to save a pretty girl like that," Anders said. Pappy just chuckled as they headed back to the fire, even bigger now, after Kick added yet more wood to the flames.

"You lookin' to bring in the whole damn Shoshone Nation, Bill?" Pappy asked, but with just enough chuckle to not get the sheriff more riled. Billy Kick ignored him and grabbed more wet cottonwood. "Not gonna be a forest within ten mile a here, you keep it up."

Corcoran made the introduction of Jeanne to the group and Jeanne in turn introduced Sandy McAuliffe. Pappy and Sandy hugged and shook hands renewing their acquaintance and everyone settled down around the fire. "Pappy shot a monster deer as we were riding back to camp, so we'll have some roasted venison coming up shortly," Bill Kick said. "Why don't you give us an idea of why you're here, McAuliffe?"

Before he could answer, Jeanne did. "I'm here because of what that bunch of men did. My pa is dead, my brother might end up a cripple, and I want to see them dead. I came here to be with you, Terrence, when you catch them."

"That ain't gonna happen," Wild Bill Kick snapped. "This

ain't no place for a little girl. You and McAuliffe ride on home in the morning, leave the outlaw catching to the men."

Before Jeanne could argue, Corcoran did. "Hold up there, pard," he said. "Jeanne's got a craw full and might just be a big help to us. How's that ankle?"

"It still aches a little," she said, "but I can walk and ride with no problem. Jeremy might lose his leg. He's got a bad infection in the bullet wound."

"We ain't turning back, sheriff," Sandy McAuliffe growled. "Been on your trail for days, two of 'em in this storm. Miss Jeanne's got it strong to see these men captured or killed, and I'm gonna be right beside her."

"I've rode with Sandy," Pappy Somerset piped up. "He's a good tracker, a good fighter, and we could use his gun. He and Jeanne would be welcome as far as I'm concerned."

Kick was standing near the fire, looking around at the group. He knew that Somerset, Corcoran, Anders, and now McAuliffe were good fighters, wouldn't let him down, and the upcoming fight with Humboldt Charley would be deadly from the word go. What was Corcoran thinking, wanting to bring a little girl in.

"I don't want no damn little girl riding with us," Kick said, again. "Ain't no place for a girl. We're talking killers, rapists, the meanest men you can imagine." He stormed about in the snow and mud, kicked some more rocks. "Ain't no place for a little girl."

"I ain't no little girl, mister," Jeanne said, quietly. "I've worked right next to my pa and the cowboys on our ranch, trained horses, shot maverick cattle, and fought with these outlaws we're looking to catch. I'm riding with Terrence."

"Yes, she is," Terrence said. "Pappy's riding for Marshal Tetford in Belmont, I'm riding for Jim Seagram in Eureka, and you're the Elko County Sheriff, Wild Bill. We're all riding for this young lady who suffered horrible abuse at the hands of Humboldt Charley. Yes, we're all riding for Jeanne Moss and she's riding with us." The fire in her eyes stayed bright but the scowl on her face slowly turned into a grand smile as Corcoran gave his little speech.

Sheriff Bill Kick had his temper up but also saw there was no room for more argument. If Kick pulled out, only Anders would ride out with him, maybe, and Corcoran would take the group in and wipe out the Humboldt Charley gang, but he wouldn't have the pleasure of that or of taking Dean Whitaker into custody. Besides all that, the gal had already faced more cruelty than any woman should ever have to, she should get her chance to see her tormentors get their come-uppance.

"All right, dammit. Corcoran, you keep her out of the way. Girl, if you cause trouble, it will be the last trouble you ever cause."

"Don't be threatening me, sheriff," she said. "I'll not be getting in your way; don't you get in mine." Her eyes were blazing as she said that. Her little fists were doubled up, her chin jutted out, and her shoulders were squared as if to swing a mighty uppercut. "And, I'll thank you to call me by name." She said this and the men for the most part were glad she was speaking to Kick and not to them. George Anders sat on his blanket, eyes wide open, as well as his mouth, hoping above all that she would be riding with them.

I've never met anyone like this in my life. I bet she would fight a she-bear or a mountain lion if thought she was right. So pretty, too. I'll ride for her, yes, I will.

Kick couldn't remember the last time he let anyone talk to him like that. He was thinking that if she was a man she would already be on her butt with a sore jaw. "Don't get in the way," is all he said and turned away from the strong-willed lady.

Anders had a smile on his face, and sat next to Sandy

McAuliffe. "I'd sure like to get to know that lady a whole lot better than I do. I've heard of the Moss ranch and their fine cattle. Looks like they grow some fine women too."

McAuliffe had to smile, nodding in full agreement with the young deputy. "You might rope her, might even get her half-tied, but draggin' her to the fire is gonna be one hell of a chore, young man."

Pappy Somerset had been tending some large pieces of venison on the fire and motioned for the group to bring their plates. He had a pot of beans perking along and a second pot of coffee boiling as well. "Want to get this while it's hot, folks." He pulled a small roast onto a board and sliced great slabs of meat onto the offered plates.

"Spoon's in the bean pot, so help yourself. I've got biscuits in the Dutch oven there, so if you go hungry tonight, it's your own fault."

"I'm hungry enough to eat two buffalo and a griz, Somerset," McAuliffe said, holding his plate for a second slice of meat. "Hope there's enough for breakfast, too."

"We'll bust out of here just after sunrise," Kick said. "Tomorrow will signal the end of the Humboldt Charley gang. Nobody acts alone tomorrow. To win, we work together, and no arguments." To make his point he threw even more wood on the fire and laid out his blanket as close as he dared. His plate also held two slices of venison roast, two biscuits, and the whole thing covered in beans.

The roasted venison shared a spot on tin plates with some good beans, and flasks of whiskey kept things lively for a couple more hours. One by one, they drifted into their blankets, as close to the fire as they dared. Corcoran stayed awake for several hours then shook Anders for the next shift. Pappy had the last shift and had a good fire going when he got the group up just before sunrise.

"Did you tell Whitaker to bring whiskey when he came

back?" Buford Gamble was still upset as hell over what had happened with Enos Payson and the young girl, and then Charley telling Whitaker that he was the boss. "He might turn on us, Charley. He might run to the Elko Sheriff, you know."

Charley had been in a rage ever since Maria shot Payson and the girl. "Five of us rode into Belmont and took that bank, Gamble. Now, there's just you and me. Whitaker does what I say, or he'll die in the flames of that town of his when I burn it to the ground. Where's Maria?"

"She's in her room, crying. We need some people, Charley and soon. Word will get out that it's just us and when that happens all the law dogs are gonna start comin' our way."

"Why don't you run up to Halleck tomorrow and see what you can find. We'll winter here and now would be a good time to see if we can put some down and out men to work, eh?" and he laughed hard and loud. "We might have to kill Maria if she doesn't quit this damn crying."

"She killed her niece, Charley."

"I killed my brother. So, what? You ride out at first light and bring three or four men back with you. Take some gold with you to show. Men like gold." He got up from the kitchen table and walked down the long hallway to Maria's bedroom and Buford headed out the door for the barn to get ready for the morning ride.

Maybe I'll just take a whole saddlebag full of gold and keep right on riding, let that crazy man crawl about waiting for me. Getting' tired of watching things fall apart around our heads.

Buford had a fire lit in the potbelly stove and started to put together a pot of coffee, said nuts to that and found his flask. His anger built one swig at a time and when the flask was empty he flung it against the wall. Gamble understood he was no match for Humboldt Charley, wasn't as fast, wasn't as accurate, but still wanted to walk into that ranch house and blow the man away.

He fell onto the bunk and pulled a blanket up. "I'm just gonna keep right on ridin' tomorrow. Goodbye, Humboldt Charley," he snickered and fell asleep immediately.

Sunrise on the high desert of eastern Nevada following a major storm can be cold enough to freeze living creatures. "Let's go, roll out, mornin' tide's here." Pappy had the fire roaring, coffee was boiling, and left-over venison roast was hot and filled everyone's biscuits nicely. It was too cold to talk, and breakfast went down quickly. Saddles were cinched down tight, blankets wrapped around heavy winter coats, and horses were blowing steam.

"Gonna be a good day," Kick said. Sunshine fought its way through the cold, snow would be melting fast, and the group was ready to hit the trail. The wind blew hard enough that the road was mostly clear of snow and the riding was fast. About two hours into the ride Pappy Somerset, riding several yards in front, called back that a rider was coming. They scattered into the high brush alongside the trail and watched a single rider walk his horse down the trail. He was wrapped in a blanket, his hat pulled low on his head.

As he got closer, Kick nodded to Corcoran. "That's Buford Gamble, Charley's number one man. Wonder where he's going?"

"Not very far," Corcoran said. He nudged old Rube out onto the trail, surprising Gamble. "This the road to Humboldt Charley's camp?" he asked all friendly like. Buford Gamble was frantic, couldn't get the blanket out of the way to get his gun, spun his pony around and put spurs deep in its flank. He was a good rider, but fighting the wool blanket, working to get his revolver out, and maintain full flight was more than he could handle.

Corcoran's Rube was at a full gallop in two strides and

the big Irishman pulled his rifle and whacked Buford Gamble across the back of the head, knocking him out of the saddle. Corcoran spun Rube around and stopped him at Buford's still body. He stepped out of the saddle as Sheriff Kick and the others rode up.

"Get up, fool," Corcoran said, driving his boot into the man's ribs. "Get up, or I'll shoot you where you lie." Buford Gamble groaned and tried to sit up, found he was all tangled in his wool robe and fought it. Kick reached down and jerked him to his feet, throwing the blanket aside, and grabbing Gamble's weapon.

Pappy Somerset and Sandy McAuliffe got a little fire going from some dried sage they ripped up and Kick brought the outlaw to it. "Charley still at that ranch, Buford?"

"Don't know what you're talking about," Gamble growled, gently rubbing the back of his head, bringing his hand back with frozen blood attached. "Who's this Charley you're talkin' about?"

A big left fist, coming straight out of the shoulder, broke Gamble's nose, and spattered more blood about. The sheriff, often called Wild Bill, drew back for a second shot and Gamble shook his head. "No more," he almost whispered. "Charley's at Maria Lopez's ranch about fifteen miles back that way." He was whimpering from the effects of the two blows and had already made up his mind to run off and leave Charley.

"Who's with him?" Kick asked.

"They're all dead. Payson, Oliver, Spittin' Sam Anson. All dead except me and Charley."

"You and Charley be joinin' 'em soon enough, Gamble," Wild Bill said. He spat a wag of tobacco into the fire and paced around a bit. "What are we gonna do with him while we take out Humboldt Charley?"

"Hang the bastard," Pappy Somerset said.

"No, this is civilized country now," Kick said. "We'll let him have his trial and then we'll hang him right alongside Charley. Unless, of course, he should give us a little trouble, then we'll just shoot the sumbitch." He spat more juice, stomped his feet some to get a bit of warmth going, and glared at the outlaw. "It would be easier just to shoot you," he said.

"Looky this," George Anders said, holding a set of saddle-bags. "These are filled with gold coins. He ain't got no food, no flask of whiskey, just gold. He was runnin' off, sheriff. Sure as hell, he was runnin' off."

"Well, put that back on his horse. We gotta keep movin'." Kick said.

"We're wasting time talking about all this. Shoot him or bring him. Well, hell, we gotta take him with us, Bill," Corcoran said. "Anders, you have cuffs with you?" Anders nodded and brought out a set. "Let's cuff his right wrist to the saddle horn, tie his feet together under the horse, and bring him along to the party."

He took a quick glance at Jeanne standing just a few feet away and saw the return of fear in her face. This was one of the men who terrorized her, who did unspoken and horrible things to her. Corcoran had to use all his powers of restraint to keep from killing Buford Gamble where he stood. Instead, he walked over, slipped an arm around Jeanne's shoulder and walked her back to her horse.

"Will you look at this?" Sandy McAuliffe said, holding open one of the saddle bags Anders was about to put back on Gamble's horse. "These bags really are filled with gold coins, mostly double eagles."

"Yeah, Corcoran snarled. They robbed two banks. Charley must have the rest of the loot at that ranch." He stood next to Jeanne, quiet for just a minute. "You must be runnin' out on your partner, eh Gamble? Hell of a man, you are, attacking young girls, killing people left and right, and now, runnin' out on a partner. Scum, that's what you are."

George Anders stepped over and wrapped a robe around Jeanne, asking if she was warm enough. Corcoran smiled and took a step back, letting nature take its course. "Let's saddle up and put Humboldt Charley in irons."

"I don't want to ride close to him," Jeanne said, mounting up.

"I'll ride next to you," Deputy Sheriff George Anders smiled, nudging his horse alongside her. "I want to hear about your ranch," he said. There were gentle chuckles from several as they moved out.

CHAPTER 17

"I don't want to hear no more of your bawlin', woman. You've got gold, you're the one who killed my man and that girl, you got nothin' to cry about. I'm hungry, so fix me food or die," he said, his eyes wild, searching about for whatever spirits infect his mind. They were in the kitchen, wood in the stove crackling on a cold fall morning. Charley stormed around the large room, kicked a chair at Maria, spat on the floor, in a mad rage.

"Food or die," he said again, louder, and he shoved Maria toward the stove. For no reason, the scene struck him funny and he repeated, three or four time, "Food or die," laughing madly, shaking fist, even reaching for his side arm a time to two but not actually drawing the weapon.

Maria cringed when Charley approached, particularly after being almost shoved into the hot stove. She wanted to run but knew he would shoot her in the back. She hoped that Buford Gamble would come in from the bunkhouse and then remembered he had ridden off hours before.

It was a scene of madness Maria, watching Charley jump from his chair screaming "Food or die" over and over. He grabbed an ornate pickle caster, etched crystal in a pure silver holder and flung it at the wall, laughing madly, and the caster was followed by two gunshots into the mess. "Food or die," he screamed, flung a chair at the back door, breaking it into pieces. And then he got very quiet, hunched down a bit, gave little furtive looks around the room as if expecting something or someone.

He shuffled around the long kitchen table, found another chair, and flopped down into it as if he were exhausted. "Food or die," he mumbled, not looking at Maria but searching for who knows what. Perspiration dripped from brow, his eyes didn't seem focused, and his hand hovered menacingly near that big six-shooter.

Maria hadn't quit crying from just after she pulled the trigger of that big rifle, killing Enos Payson and the girl, Anna Rosales. "You gonna push me too far, Charley. Anna was just a baby and Payson had his hands all over her."

"She was old enough to enjoy the attention," Charley snapped. He jumped to his feet again threatening Maria, calmed a bit and sat down, glaring at her. He relaxed just a bit and said, almost conversationally, "Buford left early to bring men here, Whitaker should be here this morning. Our deal stands, woman. You've been paid. Now, I want food and I want it now."

She had great sides of bacon frying in a large cast iron pan on the stove and with her hands wrapped in some cloth, picked the pan up and flung it at Humboldt Charley, spraying the outlaw with hot bacon grease. The heavy pan hit him square in the face and knocked him back out of his chair. He screamed as he sprawled across the floor of the kitchen, fighting to wipe the burning grease from his face.

"You miserable whore," he screamed in pain, whipping his Colt and fanning three shots through the middle of Maria's breastbone. He was howling in pain, unable to see out of his right eye, and made his way to the bucket of cold water near the back door. He splashed water on his face, over and over, fighting back the effects of the bacon grease.

He tried to rub his face and came away with chunks of burned flesh, crying out in pain and fear. He saw huge blisters on his hands from the burning grease, had difficulty keeping his balance, couldn't understand why he was blind in one eye. Panic flooded his system, shock was setting in, and he drew his weapon again, looking around as if to see someone else in the room.

He found his way down the long corridor that led to the bedrooms and into Maria's where there was a mirror. "My God," he groaned, seeing that his right eye was literally fried in the socket. The skin around his left eye was hanging from a broken blister, and his vision was blurry.

Shock was setting in, blisters were bulging on his face, some broken open when he splashed water on them or rubbed his hand across them. He screamed in pain when he touched one of the blisters, the agony of the situation slowly coming into focus.

His sense of balance was failing, he lurched about the room, bouncing off the heavy bedstead, the chest of drawers, the wall. He plopped down on the bed, tried to hold his head in his hands, and howled again as pain shot through him. He tried to calm himself down, told himself to get straightened out, stood up, and careened across the room and into the wall. He was crying out in pain, angrier than he had ever been, and slowly the truth of the situation began to make itself known.

Blind in one eye, disfigured from the boiling grease burns and his gang dead, the only thing he had were those saddlebags filled with gold. The outlaw life of Humboldt Charley was ending, and he wasn't going to let that happen. "The only one who hasn't betrayed me is Buford Gamble and he'll bring me men. We'll ravage this country come spring," and he tried to laugh through the tears and pain but couldn't.

He was overwhelmed with anger, strode back into the kitchen and put three more bullets into Maria's dead body. He was in the process of reloading his revolver when he collapsed unconscious onto the floor, next to Maria, his system overwhelmed by the attack.

It was a combination of pain and the realization that he could hear a rider coming into the barnyard that brought Humboldt Charley around. He was sitting in the middle of the kitchen floor and quickly gathered his Colt, found the bullets that were dropped, and got the weapon loaded as a rider pulled up to the hitch post near the kitchen porch.

Charley scrambled to his feet, pain from the scalding, searing. "No," he cried out, over and over, as he ran his hand over his face. He was standing in the middle of the kitchen, his left hand to his face, the other holding his Colt limply at his side when Wells town marshal Whitaker walked into the kitchen.

"What the hell happened?" he said, seeing Maria's bloody body stretched out in a pool of blood, and Charley's face covered in red, dripping blisters. He gagged some when he saw the man's right eye and eyelid, fried crisp. A chair was broken in pieces, a pickle caster and its contents splashed across a wall and on the floor, a cast iron frying pan upside down on the floor, and pieces of fried bacon littering the kitchen table and floor.

Humboldt Charley raised the pistol, loaded and cocked, and tried to aim it at Whitaker. His right eye didn't exist, he tried to use his left, got confused then the anger came on in waves. He waved the revolver at Whitaker and snarled, "Just one stupid word, fat man. Just one." He didn't pull the trigger, found himself so tired, so angry, impossible to stand up. He slumped into a chair. "Did you bring whiskey?"

"Of course, Charley. I said I would. What happened?" Dean Whitaker was shaking, fear flowing free, understanding that Charley was going to kill him. Whitaker opened a cloth sack he was carrying, and brought out a bottle of whiskey. "Let me pour you a drink and then we need to tend to those burns."

None of what he saw made any sense, Charley's face burned with hot bacon grease, apparently thrown at him by his long-time lover, Maria, and the dear lady's body mutilated by half a dozen bullet holes. *Maria Lopez has protected Humboldt Charley for years, slept with him, fought with and for him. What has happened here?*

He remembered what happened just a day or two ago, when he had to help bury Enos Payson and the young girl, and how Maria just sat, forlorn, crying, sobbing on the ground at the girl's grave.

Charley wrenched the bottle from Whitaker's hands and pulled the cork, taking two big swallows of the burning rotgut. "Where's Buford?" Whitaker asked, putting the frying pan on the stove and starting to pick up the bacon mess.

"He's in Halleck lining up some people for us. What can you do about this?" he asked running his hands lightly around his face. "Bitch threw hot grease in my face. God, it hurts," he whimpered. Charley crossed his arms on the table and tried to lay his head down, jerking up as pain seared across his face. He screamed, jumped to his feet and immediately slumped back in his chair. "God, it hurts," he murmured again.

There was the slightest grin on Whitaker's face as he motioned Charley to sit still. *This bastard is under my control now. I need to keep my wits about me, need to see to it that Humboldt Charley comes out of this dead. Those bags of gold will be mine before this day is over.*

"Let's see what we can do about this." Whitaker brought

the bucket of cold water over, got some clean rags and wetted them. "I've got powders in my saddlebags Charley. Old Doc Swenson swears by them." He went out to his horse and brought a little leather-bound kit in and opened it.

When Whitaker put the wet rag on Charley's face the outlaw screamed in pain and immediately went for his gun. "No, Charley," Whitaker howled. "I'm trying to help you. If you don't let me get these blisters cleaned out, you'll die of blood poisoning, now hold still, dammit."

Charley seemed to understand but didn't put that big hog leg back into its pouch. He held it in his hand and laid his hand on the table. He was fighting to stay awake, trying to understand what was happening, wanted to kill anything and everything. He was out of energy with so much rage, so much pain, and a mind that saw demons in every shadow.

It took more than an hour, filled with howls, angry and foul language, and threats of death before Dean Whitaker, perspiration pouring from every inch of his body stepped back. "If you keep screwing with it, Charley, you're gonna die. Drink some whiskey to ease the pain."

Whitaker reached for the bottle to pour drinks and Charley grabbed it to drink again straight out of the bottle. "Bury that bitch out there and get this place cleaned up Whitaker." Charley took the bottle and lurched out of the kitchen, apparently for one of the bedrooms and Whitaker was left to do what needed to be done.

Sure, Charley. I'll bury the lovely Maria. Yes, Charley, I'll clean the kitchen. And, oh, by the way, Charley, I'm going to kill you the first chance I get. It had started as such a simple thing a few years ago. Humboldt Charley would pay Whitaker to allow he and the gang to winter in the area and in turn, Charley wouldn't shoot up the town or rob any of the businesses.

Whitaker's face turned black in anger as his thoughts continued. *That wasn't good enough for you, was it, you Paiute bastard. Had to have more, force me to cater to your every desire, provide you with women, with whiskey. I have you now, Charley. You drink that bottle and pass out Charley, and I'll have that gold.*

There were several more bottles in the cloth sack and he opened one. "I guess I'll never know what happened," he murmured. He sat at the table idly counting the holes in Maria's body and poured another drink. "He emptied his pistol into the poor woman. I think this is the right time to separate myself from this fool before he empties it into me."

Whitaker had two more glasses of whiskey before he dragged Maria's body out of the kitchen and across the barnyard to where the others' graves were, the ground still fresh from digging. "I'm gonna bury you nice, Maria, and then get on that horse and ride out of this country. It's been a long time since I was in San Francisco," he murmured.

Charley will empty that bottle and hopefully pass out while I'm burying this lovely lady and then he'll die. Those lovely bags of gold will get me to San Francisco in style. He set to digging with just a hint of a smile on his jowly face.

The arguments over what to do with Buford Gamble finally ended when Wild Bill Kick said, "Tie him to his horse and bring him along." Pappy wanted the deputy to take him back to Elko, Sandy McAuliffe wanted to hang him on the spot, and both had supporters.

"Can't hang him," George Anders chuckled. "Ain't no trees around here."

"Can't take him back," Corcoran said. "We need Anders' gun." Kick got a little grin when he commented, "Might leave him here with Jeanne." Kick was shushed immediately.

It was a quiet ride for the first couple of hours and then a combination of warm fall sunshine and beautiful country worked its magic and tempers cooled, friendly conversation returned, and planning for the attack took front seat.

Gamble told them that when he left only Charley and the woman were at the ranch, but Whitaker was expected.

"Isn't it amazing, Deputy Anders, that when you shove the cold barrel of a Colt Peacemaker into a man's mouth and cock the hammer back, the man wants to tell you all kinds of good stories?" Corcoran laughed, nudging the young deputy with an elbow. "He couldn't get the words out fast enough, could he. It's called gentle persuasion, Anders."

"Thank you, Mr. Corcoran," Anders said in gentlemanly mockery. "I'll be sure to remember that. Do you really believe him, though? Seems he was awfully fast to tell us anything we wanted to know."

"I don't think our Mr. Gamble is smart enough to know how to lie out of this situation. He is slippery, though, Anders. Keep a close eye on him, make sure those cuffs are tight and the knots are secure."

They rode through rolling hills filled with stands of piñon and cedar, some cottonwood where there was water, and good grass. What little snow that was left from the storm melted off, they found they were riding through patches of mud from time to time.

"We'll do a quick survey of the ranch from that ridge we were on, Pappy," Corcoran said. "Should be able to tell if Charley has any guests. I think we could probably come in from three or four different directions and make him surrender. I really would like to bring him in alive."

"You know the place, Corcoran, so you plot it out for us," Billy Kick said. "But I think splitting up into three or four groups isn't gonna work. Can't talk or see to get directions. Just two groups."

"Okay, Bill, I think you're right. Pappy, you lead half and I'll lead the other half of us. Both of us have been there and know the lay out. Jeanne, you and George Anders are with me, Pappy, you take the rest."

"No," Sandy McAuliffe said. "Anders should be with the sheriff and I will be with Jeanne."

Both Terrence Corcoran and George Anders wanted to argue, but it was Pappy Somerset who won the argument. "I want you to be with me and Sheriff Kick, Sandy. We've done these things before and can work well together. Terrence has the full trust of Jeanne and believe me, young Anders isn't gonna let anything happen to her."

The only person not laughing was Buford Gamble listening to the group plot the end of Humboldt Charley. *I've got to get away from this and that girl is the answer. If I can get free of these handcuffs I can get that knife out of my boot. First chance I get I'm gonna take it.* Gamble knew he couldn't go up against either Corcoran or Anders in a fight since he didn't have his gun, but a knife to Jeanne Moss's neck would keep those two out of the way.

By the time they reached Maria's ranch what little snow was left was in the shadows and crevices and the day was warm and sunny. Pappy led Sandy and the sheriff around toward the high ridge while Corcoran led Jeanne and Anders straight up the main road to the ranch. Corcoran had the lead rope and was trailing Gamble's horse.

"You'll have the best view, Pappy," Corcoran said. "We'll get in position to attack but you'll have to give the signal from that ridge. It'll take you a good half hour to get around and up onto that ridge, so we'll settle down as close to the main house as we dare get. Let's not be doing any wild shootin' at shadows. Make sure you know who your target is. Let's get 'em."

As Corcoran led his little group, he motioned Anders close. "We got to tie this fool up tight when we get up to that ranch. We got to keep him far enough back that he can't give Charley any kind of warning. If he starts trying to yell or scream, bash him a good one."

Corcoran looked over at Gamble. "You make one little sound, make one little dumb move, and I'll use this big knife of mine on your throat, Mr. Gamble. After what you did to that beautiful little girl, I really want to kill you, make you hurt long and hard, but I believe in the law, sir. So, if you give me the slightest reason to think that you're trying to escape or hurt any one of us, you will die."

"After Corcoran kills you, Gamble, I will," Anders chuckled, holding his horse back a bit so he could ride alongside Jeanne. "Don't you get yourself in the line of fire when we get up there. You stay back and hide yourself in the trees." He gave her the biggest smile he could generate, and she returned it with pleasure.

"I want to see that horrible Charley dead and I want to see that man there dead, and I won't do anything to get in your way, George. Sandy gave me a knife when we left Eureka and I've got it strapped to me under my coat. I've cleaned enough animals that I know how to use it. Don't you worry about me, George Anders.

"You stay with Terrence Corcoran and get those men. You get them."

CHAPTER 18

WHITAKER WAS AT LEAST ONE HUNDRED POUNDS OVERWEIGHT, hadn't raised a hand in physical work beyond pulling himself closer to a table full of food, and was having a most difficult time digging a grave for Maria. He'd whack at the ground with a pick for two swings and take a break. Whack two more times and take a break. Then try to shovel what he whacked before taking another break, sweat pouring from his rotund body.

His language was as vulgar as had been heard on that ranch in many years, telling the world what he thought of Humboldt Charley, the Wells township, Elko County, and Nevada rocks. It would have been comic if the situation was any different.

He was barely down three feet when he rolled Maria's almost stiff body into the hole and took three breaks, each with a healthy swig of whiskey, shoveling the dirt and rocks over her. He struggled back into the kitchen and splashed most of the large bucket of water to cool off, poured another full glass and whiskey and sat down, exhausted.

Whitaker was smart enough to realize that he was in a position to be able to make that trip to San Francisco without a worry in the world. He had spent hours planning his getaway while digging that grave. *There's a fine reward on Humboldt Charley's head and I have him. All I have to do is walk in that bedroom down the hall and shoot the bastard. Drag his worthless body back to Wells and wire the sheriff in Elko that I got him. I can claim Payson, too. That will set me up. I'll have those bags of gold and after collecting the reward, pick them up and take a fine coach ride on steel rails to San Francisco.*

Thought of Hawaii, maybe even a tour of the Orient, and grand tables filled with the delicacies of the world were dancing in his alcoholic haze. "I've never shot a man in cold blood," he murmured, sipping a little more whiskey. "Ah, but this isn't a man, this is Humboldt Charley, a mad killer, and I'll be the hero."

As he sat at the table filling another tumbler of whiskey he remembered what Charley had said about Buford Gamble coming back with some me. "I can't wait," he mumbled. "I've got to get moving before Gamble gets back. Got to kill that man and get him to Wells." He sloshed whiskey in the glass and drank it down.

Whitaker knew his plan was a good one. Kill Humboldt Charley, drag the body and the gold back to Wells, hide the gold, and wire the Elko sheriff, get that reward, and ride the train to San Francisco. The plan was right, the man wasn't. Whitaker was terrified of Charley and wasn't sure he would be able to shoot the man in cold blood. *What if I didn't kill him? What if he came after me? What if Gamble finds out what I've done?*

Pappy led Sandy and the sheriff around the rocky ridge and they tied their horses in a stand of aspen. "From the top of that ridge up there, we can look right down on the ranch. We need to keep our heads down when we get up there. It's a bit of a scramble." The side of the hill was dotted in a few places with sage and rabbit brush and the rest was rock and shale, and the men had to use their hands as much as their feet to get up the steep hillside.

"You weren't joshin' about scramble, Somerset," McAuliffe chuckled, tucking in behind a large rock formation at the top of the ridge. There was a saddle in the middle of the ridge and they settled in for a good look at the ranch spread out before them.

"Looks like Whitaker with the shovel, sheriff." Pappy was the first to the top and was laid out behind the top of the ridge. "Looks to be digging yet another grave." Somerset snickered a bit watching the fat old man using the pick for a stroke or two and then resting some.

Billy Kick had his spyglass out and was looking from behind his own rock. "That, my friends, is the Wells town marshal. One Dean Whitaker, friend and benefactor of Humboldt Charley. And," he emphasized, "soon to be my prisoner.

"That body lying there, that will go in the hole he's digging, is Maria Lopez. This is her ranch."

"Terrence and I watched them dig those two other graves just a couple of days ago, sheriff. I wonder why everyone's getting killed down there? We heard one shot and watched them bring two bodies out. That Maria was wailing in grief when a young girl was buried. Now it's her turn to go in the ground.

"We got Buford Gamble, saw Payson get buried. Only one left is Humboldt Charley. We might just as well ride on down there and take him out, Kick."

Sheriff Kick was using his telescope to search all around the ranch house, the barn, corrals, and nearby pastures. "No other activity at all. No cattle, no cowboys, no horses in the corrals. You don't suppose Whitaker killed all those people? I can't picture that fat sumbitch goin' up against Charley."

They watched Whitaker drag Maria's body into the grave

and trudge to the ranch house. "Let's signal Corcoran to close in and we'll work our way off this ridge. We are gonna be in plain sight all the way down," Kick said.

"See that little secondary ridge to your right, sheriff? We can stay low and move down that rill right into the corral nearest the house." He pointed out the little depression in the side of the hill, and signaled to where he thought Corcoran would be to move in.

"I'm really scared, Terrence," Jeanne Moss said, sitting on the ground as close to Corcoran as she could get. "Don't leave me back here with that man." Corcoran and Anders had tied Buford to a tree, so he was facing away from the ranch and had a bandanna shoved into his mouth and tied off.

"I can't bring you with us when we attack that house, Jeanne. It would be far more dangerous than babysitting this fool." Corcoran saw Pappy Somerset waving his broad brimmed hat from behind a big rock slab high on the ridge to his south. "They're getting ready to come down now."

"I can't stay with him, Terrence. I can't," she cried. Visions of what Gamble and the other men had done raged through her mind, and Corcoran could see tears well and brake free. She threw her arms around the big man. "Please."

He could feel her whole body shaking in terror and held her tight, brushing her hair back, rocking ever so slightly. What he wanted to do was ease her away, walk over and shoot Buford Gamble dead. He thought Anders was right suggesting they hang the bastard when they found him.

"It's okay, Jeanne. You come with us, but stay well back," he whispered, feeling the intensity of her fear. "Don't get too close, cuz there's gonna be bullets flying. I'll go first, George, you come behind me and to my right, and Jeanne, hold back some and follow. Let's go."

She let herself free from the big man, nodded, and wiped away the tears. "I'll do what you want," she murmured, and watched as they moved toward the big house. She let them get a few feet in front and then moved forward also.

They were maybe thirty yards from the front of the hours and watched the sheriff bring his group down the rocky hillside toward the corrals. "Sure, wish I knew the layout of that house," Corcoran murmured. He figured the main entrance led into the great room and the kitchen would probably be behind that. "The way the building spreads north, must be where bedrooms are."

He was talking to himself as much as to Anders. "Get behind those trees there, Jeanne, and stay there." He pointed at a large locust tree and watched her get down on her haunches and out of sight.

"George, let's take a look in those windows. When Kick comes through that kitchen door we have to be coming in the front." They snuck up toward the broad veranda and across the porch. The covered porch spread the length of the building and Corcoran guessed the doorways he saw toward the north led into bedrooms, probably with another door that opened onto a hallway inside the building.

Jeanne, tucked behind the ancient locust tree watched Corcoran and Anders scurry up to the windows along the west side of the large ranch house. They tried not to make noise as they moved across the porch to the windows. Corcoran could see right through the great room and into the kitchen.

"That's Whitaker with the glass," he whispered to Anders. "See Charley anywhere?"

"No." They watched Whitaker finish the glass of whiskey and pull his revolver to check the loads. "What's he up to?" Anders was crouched low on his haunches looking in the window when Jeanne Moss screamed. He spun around and saw Buford Gamble grab her by the arm.

He had a good size knife in one hand and Jeanne in the

other. She was twisting, kicking, hitting him with her other hand, and screaming in terror. Anders was off the porch in one leap, his revolver in hand, and fired, sending a bullet across the man's shoulder, ripping some skin, but not knocking him down.

Gamble howled when the bullet tore out a large chunk of shoulder but didn't lose his grip on Jeanne. She thrashed around, got one arm under her coat, found that big knife that Sandy McAuliffe had given her and pulled it free. Gamble had her other arm in a vice grip and she spun, drove the knife all the way to the grip into his side. He let go of her arm, staggered back and fell to the ground behind the locust.

Corcoran ran and grabbed Jeanne and got her back onto the porch. He had the big Colt out and cocked. Jeanne had her arms so tightly wrapped around the big man that he wouldn't have been able to shoot if he had to. "We both frisked him, Anders. Where did he have that knife?"

"I don't know, Corcoran, but I bet that shot and all the howling has woke the dead."

Gamble was bleeding bad, the knife driven deep into his body. He tried to crawl around the tree, to see where Corcoran and the others were. He still had hold of his knife, but didn't have any other weapon. All he could think about was escape. He crawled back to where the horses were, trying to use that big tree to hide his movements.

"Check and make sure he's dead, Anders," Corcoran said, getting Jeanne calmed down and out of sight on the veranda. "You stay down as low as you can, Jeanne. Whitaker is inside the house and sheriff Kick and them will be crashing into the kitchen at any minute."

"He's not here," Anders shouted from behind the Locust. He saw a trail of mashed leaves covered in blood leading back toward the horses. "He's going for the horses," he howled, running, following the trail of blood. He broke through a stand of sage in time to see Gamble on a horse, running off.

"Come on," Corcoran yelled at Jeanne, grabbing her arm and running hard through the brush and trees for where the horses were. He thrust Jeanne into Anders's arms, jumped on Rube, and raced after Gamble. "Protect her," he yelled.

His pistol was loaded and cocked, his nerves frayed, and his whiskey courage in place as Whitaker moved from the kitchen to the corridor that led to the bedrooms. *There's two on each side of the hallway, and Maria's is the last one on the right. I bet Charley's in there.* He reached the open door to Maria's room and slowly entered, the pistol ready to fire at the slightest sound or movement. Charley was spread-eagle on his back, snoring gently, an empty whiskey bottle alongside.

Whitaker took two steps into the room, raised the weapon when a gunshot echoed through the ranch house. He spun at the sound and Humboldt Charley came straight up, his Colt out. "What the hell's going on?"

Whitaker spun back around to face Charley, both men pointing fully cocked weapons at each other. "Gunshot," is all Whitaker said.

Charley's one eye narrowed as he seemed to understand the situation. Why was Whitaker in his room with a drawn weapon? Who was outside firing a gun? Charley's mind was slowed by that bottle lying empty, but he sensed danger from Whitaker. "Whatever you say better be good, fat man," Charley growled. Before Whitaker could speak they heard the kitchen door splintered open and pounding boots thundering into the house.

Charley fired twice before Whitaker could even budge, putting two large chunks of lead into the man's chest. He stumbled backward and as he fell, he fired his weapon once. Charley screamed as the bulled tore through his arm, entering near the wrist and exiting at the elbow. Bone, flesh, and blood spewed from the horrible wound. Charley dropped his gun from the shock and rolled off the bed, writhing in pain.

He ripped a sheet from the bed to help stem the blood, but it wouldn't stop, and he pressed on the wound as hard as he could. His vision, already drastically impaired, was wavering now from the added pain and shock of the bullet wound. He managed to get back on his feet, found the dropped weapon, and waited for whatever was going on in the house. He hoped the noises he heard was Gamble coming back with men for his gang.

Kick, Somerset, and McAuliffe were less than ten feet from the back door of the ranch house when they heard Anders' gunshot. "Let's go," the sheriff shouted, racing to the door and throwing his entire weight into it. The door splintered and fell away from the hinges as the three men raced into the kitchen.

Kick moved through the large kitchen and into the great room, stopping when two gunshots echoed down the hallway. He bounded for the hallway when another shot rang out followed by a loud scream.

"Sounds like somebody might be hurt down there," he quipped. He motioned for Pappy and Sandy to follow him and he edged slowly down the corridor. "Nice and slow, boys. Somebody's hurt, and there's more than just Charley back there."

Howls of pain led the way and Kick carefully looked into Maria's bedroom. Humboldt Charley was on the bed, screaming in pain, blood pumping from both ends of the gunshot while Whitaker was slumped against the wall on the floor, bleeding to death.

Pappy Somerset whipped Charley's weapon away from the side of the bed and grabbed some sheet to try and stop the bleeding. "It ain't gonna stop," he muttered, and watched

Charley slowly drift away in his fetal position and bleed out. "What the hell happened to his face? Will you look at that?" Pappy was a strong man, fought in some big Indian campaigns, and horrible wounds were not something new to the man.

"I've never in my life seen wounds as terrible as these are." The old tracker was bent over considering Humboldt Charley's face. "His eye and lids are boiled, fried, as if someone threw hot grease in his face. Horrible," he said, and stepped back.

Kick gave a cursory look but said, "Where's Corcoran?" He ran back up the corridor and out the front door just as George Anders was leading Jeanne Moss up to the porch.

"Gamble got away," Anders said. "He got himself untied, grabbed Jeanne, but she drove a knife in him. He stole a horse and Corcoran is chasing him right now."

Jeanne ran to Sandy McAuliffe and wrapped her arms around the old man, sobbing. "I used your knife, Sandy. It was horrible, but I did like you said. I held it as tight as I could and just drove it in. It went in all the way," she cried. "I've had to take care of animals on the ranch, killed steers, lambs, goats, deer, but this was different.

"Sandy, I tried to kill that beast. That's what he is, a beast. He had his knife ready to slit my throat and George shot him and then I stabbed him. Oh, God, Sandy, I was so scared."

"You did fine, Jeanne," he said, patting her on the back. She stood back and looked at him. "I'd do it again, too, if I had to."

"Pappy, you and Sandy stay here and take care of Jeanne. George, let's go." Kick and Anders ran to the horses and grabbed the two remaining horses. "Looks like they lit off down the main road," the sheriff yelled, putting the spurs to his mount.

They rode hard for about fifteen minutes and pulled their

horses up to let them blow. At a walk, Kick had George tell him what had happened. "How did Gamble get free? I've seen some of the knots you've tied, Anders."

"I don't know, sheriff. Unless he was able to get to that knife. You frisked him and didn't find the knife. It's a big one, too. Must have had it tucked down his pants or something."

"You were right, George. We should have just hung the bastard when we caught him. Bringing him back with us was a mistake, and you give me a good jab if I try to make another one down the line."

Anders had to chuckle at that knowing full well he would never bring the subject up again. "What's done is done, sheriff," is all he said, and they nudged their horses into a gentle lope, following the obvious trail left by Gamble and Corcoran, which led them out of the narrow draw from the ranch.

They put their horses in a fast trot moving out of the rolling hills and onto the valley floor. "At this rate, we'll be back at the Humboldt Wells before long," Kick said. They saw dust billow up about half a mile to their right and turned into the brush to check it out.

Within just a few minutes they rode up on Corcoran tying Gamble's body onto the back of a horse. "Got him, did you?" Kick asked stepping off his horse.

"No, Jeanne did," Corcoran smiled. "He bled out from her knife wound. Look at this thing she's been carrying." He held out the bloody knife for Kick and Angers to see. "He had one too, and cut the ropes he was tied with."

"Don't want to mess with a woman what carries a knife like that one," Billy Kick laughed. "You been making moon eyes at that gal, better make sure you know what you're doing there." Anders chuckled, but gave the sheriff's words some thought just the same.

They mounted and started the long ride back to the ranch.

"It's over, Jeanne. Humboldt Charley is dead." She couldn't stop her sobbing, couldn't put away the vivid pictures of her torment, couldn't stop shaking, and just let Sandy McAuliffe hold her tight. "You'll be fine," he said, easing her to her feet. "Let's go inside and I'll make us some coffee."

She took in the shambles of the room as he got her comfortable at the kitchen table, stirred the fire and got coffee boiling when Pappy Somerset walked in. "That's the ticket. Jeanne, your bad guys are no more. You have nothing to fear from them." He sat down next to her and held her hand, gently rubbing her knuckles. "Terrence Corcoran and Billy Kick will catch Gamble I'm sure. You're one tough lady. Old Bill Moss would be proud, girl."

"I don't feel very tough, Pappy. I want to go home. Take me home." They sat at the kitchen table drinking coffee until well after sunset. Pappy had walked back up that rocky ridge and brought their horses down to the ranch and tucked them into one of the corrals.

"Guess we'll never know the full story about what happened here over this last several days," McAuliffe said. "Bodies being buried beside the barn, the town marshal and Humboldt Charley killing each other, and him mutilated. Looks like a bull and a bear got into it here in the kitchen." That brought laughter from Jeanne for the first time in days.

"Corcoran should be coming back, I would think," Sandy said, "unless they have to chase Buford Gamble all the way back to Elko. I'm gonna search out some food for us, Pappy. We left everything back at our camp this morning."

It took an hour or more to put together a good supper and they were finishing up a pot of beef and beans when Corcoran, Kick, and Anders rode up to the front of the ranch house. "You boys almost missed supper," Pappy joshed as they came in.

"I'm not one to miss a meal, old man," Billy Kick said, slipping out of his winter coat. "Cold out there."

The large pot of meat and beans was history in a matter of minutes and the group sat at the table, thoughts about what happens next in everyone's face. It was Sandy McAuliffe who broke the ice. "What do we do now?"

"Tonight, we sleep warm," Wild Bill Kick chuckled, "and tomorrow we have some nasty work to do. These bodies will all have to be brought to Wells, I'm going to have to put that charming deputy marshal Wallace Chandler under arrest and name George Anders as Wells deputy in residence for the Elko Sheriff."

"I might make a suggestion, there, Wild Bill," Terrence Corcoran said. He got up and waked to the big stove and brought the coffee pot back to the table. "Let's bring Humboldt Charley, Buford Gamble, and Dean Whitaker back to town for burial, and send Chandler and a couple of local bad boys to dig up these others and bring them in."

"That does sound like a much better idea," Pappy Somerset snorted. "Much better. I'm going to need to send wires to Belmont to make sure they know everyone's alive and well, and maybe we'll get some information back on how Jeremy's leg is doing."

"Seagram's gonna want to hear from me, also," Corcoran said.

"Sounds good to me," Kick said. "Let's get our bed rolls in, get a good fire going, and sleep in front of that fireplace."

No one said it, but everyone hoped the Elko sheriff wouldn't build another massive fire like the night before. "That stew was good, Pappy, but the roasted venison at Humboldt Wells was better," Jeanne said. "I want to go home."

CHAPTER 19

THE TROUPE RODE INTO TOWN JUST BEFORE NOON AND created a traffic-stopping scene when they pulled their horses to a stop in front of the marshal's office. Wallace Chandler stormed out the doors when he saw Whitaker's body slung across the back of his horse. "What happened?" he demanded. "Who did this?" Chandler was a selfish man and everything had to relate to him.

In this situation he thought he saw an opportunity. With Whitaker dead he might just be named town marshal. *That's the sheriff with that trouble maker Corcoran and that's Humboldt Charley's body. This might be to my benefit.*

He was a mousy little man who had trouble under-standing the concept of truth and justice, had spent years nursing the thought of replacing Whitaker. He watched closely how it was that Whitaker could keep the outlaws from pillaging Wells by giving them protection. Watched Whitaker bend his knee to Humboldt Charley, and now, here's Charley spread across a saddle right next to the marshal. *No more Charley, no more Whitaker, and I just might get that badge for myself.* He puffed himself up, strutted over to look at the bodies, and demanded again, "Who killed Marshal Whitaker? Who's responsible for this outrage?"

"Chandler," Elko Sheriff Billy Kick barked, "You're under arrest." Corcoran had stepped behind the snarly deputy and lifted the revolver from his holster. "Your days of protecting and serving the outlaws of this territory are over." He looked around to see the street filled with locals getting a good view. He tipped his hat to several in the crowd and did his best to hide just the slightest smile that kept trying to edge into view. It was a good day for the Elko County Sheriff.

"You can't do this," Chandler said. He puffed up, almost swaggered, saying, "I'm deputy town marshal here. You have no authority to arrest me."

"You're looking down the barrel of his authority," Corcoran snickered. "Of course, if you want, I can give you your gun back and you can try to go up against all of us. Might just like that, eh boys?"

"Go ahead," Sandy McAuliffe said. "Give it back to that fool. I ain't shot nobody in a couple of hours, and need the practice." The crowd loved it and cheered the old mountain man. McAuliffe, still mounted, turned to the crowd, nodded gently, and turned back to Chandler. "Don't seem to have much back up, deputy."

"Okay," Wild Bill Kick chuckled. "Playtime is over." He reached out and snatched Chandler by the front of his shirt and shoved him back to where the horses were tethered speaking to Chandler and , to the crowd in the street.

"Those bodies you're looking at are dead criminals, outlaws, murderers, and one dumb ass and piss poor lawman who worked for them. That, my friends, is the feared Humboldt Charley and what's left of his gang. The rest of his gang is buried at Maria Lopez's ranch north of town. And you," and he sashayed Chandler from horse to horse, "are the only living member of that gang."

He shoved Chandler's face right up to the mangled face of the dead Humboldt Charley, then jerked him over to Whitaker's dead bloat, and finally to the bloody mess that once was Buford Gamble.

"Get that pig in a cell and let's get on with our work," Kick said, all but dismissing the crowd. Corcoran and the rest jammed their way into the office and Chandler was slammed into one of the cells in the back. Sandy McAuliffe put some wood in the potbelly stove and got a pot of coffee started. "I do believe we just might have another storm brewin' out there. My bones ache some."

"Called age, not a storm," Pappy Somerset laughed. "Mine ache every day. What are we gonna do with those bodies, sheriff?"

"George, you and Jeanne stay here in the office, Pappy, you and Corcoran have some wires to send out, and McAuliffe, let's you and me see if we can find some willing residents to see that Mr. Chandler is able to get those bodies back to town for decent burial.

"Better get those bodies over to the undertaker, too," Billy Kick said. "It's been a long few days, so let's get these little jobs done and then we'll meet back here first thing in the morning."

Corcoran chuckled thinking, the command structure was established in the township of Wells, Nevada. He and Pappy headed down Main Street to the telegraph office located in the railroad depot. The wind was blowing up a storm of leaves and dust and carried the feel of another blast of early winter was on the way. "I think Sandy's bones were telling the truth, Terrence."

"With the gold we found in Gamble's saddlebags and the gold in all those bags at the ranch, it doesn't look like much was spent. The banks will be glad to get it back."

"There'll be a big fight over it, you can bet," Pappy chuckled. "That Belmont banker is sure to claim it all and you can bet the Eureka banker will too." He opened the door to the telegraph office and felt the heat from the wood stove immediately. "That feels good. Think they'll have coffee too?"

Pappy sent a short note to Tetford in Belmont saying that Jeanne Moss was safe, the bank's money had been recovered, and the Humboldt Charley gang was no more. Corcoran's note to Sheriff Seagram in Eureka was almost the same and they said it felt very much like time for a cold beer.

"Do you suppose that feller, Lody Sparkman would pour a couple of cold brews for the likes of us?" Pappy asked. With a vigorous nod from Corcoran, the two came through the batwing doors of the Golden Globe Saloon.

"I do believe he will."

"Saved the day again, eh Corcoran?" Lody laughed. "Nice catch."

"I think you'll be seeing some changes around this old town my friend. The days of Dean Whitaker playing host to the outlaws is over. Would you have a wee bit of Kentucky tucked away?"

Several of the men that were in the saloon gathered around, wanted to know what was going on and what was being said. The old town hadn't had any excitements since Charley shot the deputy. And this kind of activity was good for the saloon business. Sparkman primped himself up, carried the finest barman smile, and knew if Corcoran and Pappy Somerset stayed around some, he'd have a good bar.

Stories like bringing the dead bodies of Charley and Whitaker right through town, arresting the deputy town marshal in front of the whole town, and just walking off into the office and leaving the bodies out in the street would be good for business for at least a week.

Sparkman reached under the bar for a crystal decanter, not on the shelf behind the bar for rotgut, and poured for the two men. "I snuck out to take a look at Charley when you boys brought him in. What happened to that man? Those were burns on his face."

"They were," Corcoran said. "Near as we can figure, Charley must have done something to get Maria Lopez pretty upset." He chuckled just a bit and took of sip of good whiskey. "Must have thrown a frying pan full of hot grease in his face. The Humboldt Charley outlaw days ended by way of fried pig."

There was general laughter through the smoky saloon and more than one feller raised his glass to the thought. "Here's to the fried pig that done in old Humboldt Charley," an inebriated old timer shouted to many cheers and hoorahs. It was a crowd ready for a party and there was a gentleman standing at the bar, Irish in descent who loved a good party.

"This is sippin' whiskey," Corcoran said, "so I think I'll just stay and sip a while."

Jeanne Moss and George Anders were sitting in old cane back chairs across from each other at the town marshal's desk sipping coffee. "I slept well last night, but I'm absolutely exhausted," she said. "I feel like my pa's wind up clock near the fireplace when he winds it too tight and it squeals."

"Are you gonna squeal some?" Anders chuckled, and Jeanne laughed at the thought. "You've been through more than anyone ever should have to go through. If you want to squeal, it's okay with me." He saw a combination of anger and sorrow in the set of her mouth, her hair was a tangled mess, but her eyes were warm and friendly, and a smile came slowly on. George Anders had never seen a more beautiful woman in his young life.

"You're a very nice man, George Anders. If you hadn't shot that horrible man he would have killed me. I haven't had a chance to thank you for that," she said, lowering her eyes and giving him a broad smile."

Anders was raised on a large cattle ranch north of Elko and came by wearing a badge almost by accident, having busted up an attempted hijack of a stagecoach. Wild Bill Kick came up short a deputy and talked Anders into taking the job. He wanted to get back to cattle ranching.

This is the most charming and lovely girl I've ever met in my life. I wonder if she would let me escort her back to her ranch? Several days on the trail, I'd know if I really wanted to be with her forever. I sure do want to find out.

"Are you going back to your ranch right away?"

"Just as soon as I can," she said. "With pa dead and Jeremy all busted up, I've got to get back. The men should have the herds down and they will need me to tell them which groups of cattle should go in which winter pastures. They gotta be separated for market, there's branding to be done, culling of the old ones. Pa and I have it all mapped out, but they don't know that.

"Funny, isn't it? With all those fine cowboys we hire pa always acted like I was the cow boss, but I know I wasn't. But that ranch needs me, and I need that ranch really bad right now." George could see tears well up but they didn't spill. She stiffened up, squared her shoulders some and took a long drink of coffee to quell the possibility of crying in front of this nice fella.

"You and your pa were really close, eh?" George was almost staring into her huge eyes and watched her mouth as it moved from serious to smiling, and knew he would never meet another girl like this ever.

"We've always done everything together around the ranch. Jeremy isn't as strong as most boys or young men and pa depended on me a lot. I'll probably leave for home in the morning."

He wanted to say something about escorting her home, wanted to ask her many more questions, wanted to spend the rest of his life watching her lovely face move through various emotions. That ended when Billy Kick and Sandy McAuliffe stormed through the doors of the office.

Kick grabbed the cell keys and marched into the jail area at the back of the building and brought Wallace Chandler out of his cell. "Got a little job for you, Chandler. There's three men out front gonna escort you to the Lopez ranch and you and them are gonna bring those dead bodies back to town. One of the men is a deputy sheriff and I've given him explicit instructions to shoot you first if there's any trouble. You and the other two will do the diggin'. Now, git," he said, opening the door and shoving the man out onto the boardwalk.

The deputy, a man of about forty years, long, thin, and with an angry look about him, was sitting on a fine gelding, a fine lever action rifle resting comfortably across the pommel, and two men were in a wagon pulled by two up. Chandler climbed in the back of the wagon and the group started off for the Lopez place. "Bring 'em all back, dead or alive, deputy," Kick chuckled, waving them off.

Johnny Bedient, that new badge riding prominently on his blanket coat, waved back to the sheriff. Bedient had been a deputy in Elko before quitting and moving to Wells to open a hardware and gun shop, and told Kick many stories over the years about how Whitaker and Chandler operated. "Sure, Wild Bill, I'll take my old badge back for a few days. Glad you cleaned out this den of thieves."

Kick stepped back into the office. "Let's hit that café over there. I'm hungry enough to tackle a whole buffalo."

"Was that Johnny Bedient riding shotgun on those men?" George Anders asked. "I think you hired me when he quit."

"Yup," Connors said. They walked into the restaurant and found a table near the front windows. "Smells mighty good in here."

Kick, Anders, Sandy McAuliffe, and Jeanne Moss settled

in and Angie Bonét brought them menus. "We're a hungry bunch, miss," Sandy said. "I think you might need some help bringing all the food we're gonna order up."

Angie laughed and pulled out her pad and pencil. "I fed Corcoran and Somerset, so I won't have any trouble feeding your bunch. Where are those two scallywags, anyway?"

"More'n likely, got their bellies nestled mighty close to a bar," Kick chuckled. "How about steaks and potatoes and apple pie and coffee all the way around."

"It's on its way," she said, almost dancing back toward the kitchen. *I hope Corcoran's gonna be here for more than just tonight. That man can dance*, and she arrived in the kitchen blushing, remembering the other things Corcoran could do.

"Were you serious about me staying here in Wells as the resident deputy?" George Anders was sitting at the desk in the marshal's office talking with Sheriff Kick. They had sent Jeanne and McAuliffe back to their hotel after supper.

"I was very serious, George. You're a fine man, a good law dog, and it's obvious this little town hasn't had one for some time. Something you want to talk about?"

"Well, you gave the badge back to Johnny Bedient and I was just wondering."

"There's something on your mind, Anders. Spit it out, boy." Wild Bill Kick thought he knew but was going to force Anders to say it right out.

Anders got up and walked over to the stove, threw some wood in, poured a cup of coffee and sat back down, not saying a word. Kick just stood by the desk watching, tapping a toe on his right foot. "Well," Anders stammered. "Miss Moss is leaving in the morning for that long ride back to her ranch and all," and he kind of let his sentence trail off to nowhere.

"And you think that you want to be her escort to that big Moss Ranch in the Monitor Valley," he chuckled.

"Um, uh, yeah," he almost whispered.

"And you want me to ask Johnny Bedient to remain as deputy until you get back from this wonderful job of escorting a beautiful girl across Nevada's great wasteland."

"Uh, yeah," he said again. "Sorta."

Kick had to chuckle again, poured some coffee and took one of the chairs. "Tell you what, Deputy Anders, here's the deal. You talk to Jeanne and if she is acceptable to you helping to escort her home, I'll ask Bedient to stay until you get back. He won't be back into town until late tomorrow at the earliest.

"And I talked with Pappy and Jeanne at the hotel and they ain't leaving until day after tomorrow. You have breakfast with her and let me know." Kick swilled the remains of the coffee onto the bare wood floor to join hundreds of other last drops from over the years, pulled into his heavy coat and walked toward the door, still chuckling to himself about young love and duty.

"You're sure you'll be coming back?" he asked, and not waiting for an answer walked out closing the door quickly. Anders stood near the stove with a dumb little-boy grin on his face.

No, I'm not sure I'm coming back. And another thing, Sheriff Kick, I don't want to come back.

CHAPTER 20

CORCORAN AND ANGIE BONÉT LEFT THE CAFÉ TOGETHER AND walked to where Angie said there would be good dancing music. They were listening to some of that good music coming from the large building. "What is this Grange Hall you're taking me to?" he asked.

"The Grange? You should know about that. It's where families involved in farming and ranching gather. Where've you been, Terrence?"

"Talk to me about a miner's union hall I'd know what you were talking about. That does sound like good music, though." He did a little skip or two, gathered her up and twirled her about, right on the board sidewalk. She laughed and danced right along with him, letting him grab just a bit of her cute little bottom end.

"You behave yourself, Terrence, there's people watching all this." She made him walk beside her and reached for his hand. "How long are you gonna be with us, Terrence Corcoran?" she asked. "I like dancing with you." She squeezed his hand and gave him a glorious smile.

"Well, Angie darlin', you gotta remember I'm a Eureka County deputy and I have responsibilities." He smiled down at her beautiful face and wondered, just for a minute, why he was such a wanderer. *Come home every night to such a girl? But not drinkin' and fightin' at the saloon or stable. Good food every night? But not ridin' old Rube for days at a time chasing some yahoo outlaw. Nope, Angie, darlin girl that you are, I was born to wander. Must have got that from ma and pa since I was born on the boat bringin' all of us to this country.*

"You wouldn't like me hanging around after a while. Four walls make me nervous after a spell."

He didn't have to elaborate, she could see his long answer in his eyes and the set of his jaw. "We'll dance the night away and let tomorrow worry about tomorrow," she said. "That young deputy you're riding with has eyes for that pretty girl you're riding with," she chuckled. "She doesn't smile much, though. As pretty as she is, she should be smiling all the time."

"Had some hard times," is all Corcoran said. "That feller on the harmonica seems to know what he's doin', Angie," he said as they entered the hall. The Grange Hall was an old warehouse most of the time, and used for monthly meetings and a few nights of dancing by the Grange. It was filled with people, some dancing, some sitting at tables talking, and some just milling around. It seemed to be a happy crowd and generously mixed with younger and older couples.

"They do a potluck supper and hold a meeting once a month, Terrence, and the farmers and ranchers from all around come here. It's what people that are settled do, you know," she quipped.

"Look at those paintings," Corcoran said, and she had to chuckle. The walls held several large paintings of farms and ranches, rich with animals and produce. "Might make a man want to settle down and grow some cows," he chuckled. "Or corn." Angie knew he was joshing for her benefit and kept her mouth shut.

They found a table in the large hall and he helped her out of her heavy coat. "Sounds like good music," he said. Like any good raw-boned, emotional Irishman, music was genetically a part of his life. He did indeed like to dance and they were out on the floor when he felt a heavy fist slam into his kidney. The air was driven from him, his knees went weak, and he staggered a step or two, spinning around, the big Colt flashing in the lamp light.

People were pushing and shoving to get out of the way, some women of course were screaming, and men were heard to use a bit of profanity when shoved. Angie Bonét was pushed and almost lost her balance. The one-way fight was sudden and vicious.

Before Corcoran could pull the trigger, a fist slammed into the side of his head. The Colt flew one way and Corcoran the other, falling across a table and onto the floor. Before he could get back on his feet, a boot bashed him in the head and another in the ribs. Reaction alone set in and he grabbed that boot and rolled hard. He heard the leg snap and scrambled the best he could to his feet. He was dizzy, felt he would throw up at any second, and fought to stay conscious.

Angie Bonét had quickly grabbed the big revolver and handed it to Corcoran as he tried to shake off the brutal beating. He couldn't catch his breath, couldn't see very well, and could taste his own blood.

The man with the broken leg rolled across the floor, knocking two tables over and whipped his revolver out but was slammed by two fast shots through the chest before he could pull the trigger. He slowly slumped over, letting the gun fall to the floor. Corcoran kicked it away, put his back in leather, and kneeled to look at the man.

Not a word had been spoken between them before, during, or after the brawl and Corcoran didn't recognize the dead man. "Anybody know this man?" he asked, looking around at all the faces. "Angie, you have any idea who he is?" Nobody said a word and Angie just shook her head.

Corcoran still couldn't catch his breath from the heavy blow to his kidneys and then the boot to the ribs. His jaw was moving so he didn't figure it was broken. *Damn, that's gonna hurt tomorrow. I gotta find out who this fool is and why he attacked me.*

The life of an itinerant lawman involves having contact with men of the lowest social order, hurting them, putting them in jail, wrecking their criminal way of life, and that lawman never knows when someone out of his past might show up to create trouble. Is that what this is? He wondered, looking closely at the man and not recognizing him at all.

George Anders came running at the sound of gunfire from the Grange Hall and burst through the crowd. "Corcoran," he exclaimed. "What happened?" He bent down to look at the body. "That's Arnold Pepper," he said standing back up and looking into Corcoran's face. "You shoot him?"

"Yup, surely did, George. Man attacked me and damn near got me good. You know him, eh?" Corcoran thought he might have heard the name before but wasn't sure.

"Arnold Pepper's a bank robber and murderer. Last job we know about was in Winnemucca. He usually hangs out in Silver City, Idaho. Must have been in town to meet up with Humboldt Charley and saw us bring him and Whitaker in. He's a mean one, Corcoran."

"Was," is all Corcoran said. "Arnold Pepper, eh? I've heard the name. Who'd he ride with, George?"

"Heard tell about Butch Cassidy but I don't believe it. More an Idaho outlaw. Did get into Wyoming, but seldom Nevada or Utah. Strange he would just walk in and slam you about. You carry some heavy background, Corcoran."

Corcoran grimaced at the comment, then smiled and putting his arm around Angie Bonét, said, "I need some doctoring, Angie. Think you could take care of that for me?" They were laughing and joshing each other on their way out the door.

"Let's get old Mr. Pepper off to the undertaker, boys. Everybody agree Corcoran had to shoot him?" He got full agreement from those assembled and helped get the body out the door.

"I'm gonna hurt everywhere there is to hurt come morning," Corcoran said, letting Angie lead him down the street to her little cabin. "No dancing tonight, darlin'," he said.

"There's more than one way to dance, Irish," is all she said helping him in the door. "I'll be gentle."

"Your first day on the job got busy, eh young man?" Sandy McAuliffe said when George Anders joined he and Jeanne Moss at the breakfast table. "Heard some gunfire. Anyone we know?"

"Arnold Pepper tried to take out Corcoran at the dance last night,"

Jeanne Moss cried out, "No!" She grabbed Anders by the arm as he sat down. "Terrence, oh no. Is he hurt bad?"

"Yeah, actually, he's dead," Anders said, picking up the menu.

There was absolute silence at the table. Jeanne Moss was gasping for air, her eyes wide with fear and horror at Terrence Corcoran being killed. Sandy McAuliffe found it hard to believe that anyone could take out the crazy Irishman. "How is it that the Pepper feller could come down on Corcoran like that," Sandy asked.

"No, no," Anders chuckled. "No, you got it wrong. Pepper attacked Corcoran, but Corcoran killed the bad man." Jeanne sat straight up, letting what Anders said sink in.

"Terrence is okay? He's not dead?" she all but whimpered. "Oh, my God you gave me a scare when you said that."

It was a few minutes before calm returned to the breakfast table. "Are you still planning to leave for your ranch today?" Anders asked.

"No. We were but I want to pick up a few things while I'm here, including a mule to carry everything. I think we'll leave tomorrow. I'm hoping there will be an answer to our wires from Belmont, also." She lowered her eyes, got a bit of a smile on her pretty face, and asked, "Why, George?"

Sandy McAuliffe coughed gently and stood up. "I better go see if I can find a mule for us, Jeanne. Good morning, George."

George Anders nodded to Sandy, looked at Jeanne's smiling face and was almost speechless. "I'm not very good at talking to pretty ladies," he stammered.

"You're very good at saving their lives," she said, again giving him that devastating smile. "Why did you want to know if we were leaving today?"

"Jeanne, I was raised on a cattle ranch, know cows and horses pretty good. I'm a deputy almost by accident." These weren't the words he really wanted to say and was having a devil of a time getting the right ones out. "What I mean is, well, dog gone it all, I want to help escort you home to your ranch and get to know you better. There, darn it, I said it."

Jeanne laughed softly, Anders had his chin tucked all the way to his chest, staring at the table, and she reached out and took his hand. "You have strong hands, George. I like that. You saved my life and I really like that. I would be honored if you would escort me home.

"I'd be even more pleased if you would stay for the winter and help me plan out next season's herd. We'll need to cull some heifers, need to save back some bulls, and there are some fine colts coming three that need serious training. I can't do it all, George."

He knew his heart stopped at least twice and then hammered so hard he was sure she could hear it. "My goodness," is all he said, squeezing her hand over and over, smiling into her big eyes, and stammering, "my goodness," at least three more times.

"We can ride to Elko first thing tomorrow morning, load your personal stuff on our new mule, ride to Eureka the next day to say goodbye to Sandy McAuliffe, and then it'll be two or three days to the ranch. Do you have a lot of stuff to pack?"

"No," he stammered. "Just some clothes and stuff. I've been staying at a boarding house, so no. I'm a good roper and have some good ropes. I've also got some real Spanish reatas, hand braided rawhide reatas. Ever seen one?"

"One of my hands came over from California and uses a reata. You two will get along just fine." Breakfast took a bit of time as the two young people talked, flirted, and planned.

"You gonna be able to ride, Corcoran?" Pappy Somerset was still chuckling after hearing about the previous night's activities. "Got yourself all busted up dancing with a pretty girl. Well, my, my, my. What's our plan?"

"It's hard to laugh, old man," Corcoran snarled, easing himself into a chair at the café. "I'll be lighting out for Eureka shortly. I imagine old Seagram will have plenty to say about how long I've been gone. You?"

"I'll ride with you, Corcoran. Kinda wish I was younger and could ride the trails again. This is probably my last one. I'll make it back to Belmont and old Tetford will hit me up to take a badge and I just might do it." He took a long drink of his coffee. "You got any idea why that yahoo went for you?"

"Not a one, Pappy. Not a one and it bothers me some. Humboldt Charley wasn't known to pick up just anyone to ride with him. Buford Gamble and Enos Payson had paper spread across the west and the meanest of the bunch, George Oliver was wanted everywhere.

"I don't think Pepper's attack on me had anything to do with Charley, despite what young Anders thinks."

"We'll need to keep our eyes open, riding back to Eureka. Stopping in Elko on the way?"

"Yeah, let's do that," he smiled.

Corcoran walked to the hotel and up the stairs to Jeanne Moss's room. "Hi, Jeanne. Just wanted to say goodbye. I'm glad everything turned out right for you. When are you leaving?"

"I wish you were riding with us, Terrence. I've never met a man like you and there's no way I can ever thank you enough for what you've done." She wrapped her arms around the big man and hugged tight. "We're leaving in the morning. Are you leaving right now?"

"Yeah. Pappy Somerset and I will ride to Elko, then south to Eureka. He's going to wait for you and George Anders in Eureka and ride back to your ranch with you two."

"That's good. Will we ever see each other, Terrence? I mean, down the line? I want us to be friends, always." Tears had welled and were about to course down her cheeks, and she was fighting off the sobs that could already be heard.

"Pappy has told me that whatever town you ride into some beautiful woman come running up to throw her arms around you. I want to be one of those women, Terrence."

"I love to travel, to wander through this vast land we call the west, Jeanne Moss, and one of my favorite stops, from now on, is going to be the Moss Ranch in the Monitor Valley. Yes, dear lady, we'll always be friends." He hugged her back, kissed her gently on the forehead, and stepped back into the hotel hallway. *I hope young George Anders is man enough to take care of this charming lady. How strange, all of this because I got knocked around by those Indians and took a few days off to ride through the mountains. Yes, dear Jeanne, I'll see you again and often.*

CHAPTER 21

"THOUGHT WE BETTER SAY OUR GOODBYES BILLY KICK," Corcoran said when he and Pappy Somerset walked into the marshal's office. Their horses and pack mule were tied off. "It's been a good few days. Nobody hurt bad and the bad guys done in."

Kick was alone in the office and walked to the men shaking hands and indicating the coffee was hot and fresh. "Grave robbers haven't returned yet so I'm holding down the fort," the sheriff said. "Gotta say, Corcoran, you look like hell this morning. Feel just as bad?" he snickered.

Corcoran winced pouring his coffee, tried to chuckle at the comment and found that hurt just as much. "Never saw it coming, Bill. Dancing with Angie Bonét one minute, flat on the floor the next. George said his name was Pepper. Don't know the man."

"Don't like sayin' it, but I guess I gotta. It's been good ridin' with you, again, Terrence," Wild Bill Kick said with just a hint of a grin. He poured himself a cup and sat back down in the rocker behind the desk. "By the way, does the name Ladd mean anything to you?"

"Bronco Johnny Ladd," Corcoran said. "Put him away a

few years ago. Cattle rustler worked up and down the Snake River in western Idaho Territory. What about him?"

"He's out and that's why Pepper was after you. Bronco Johnny's put a claim out on you. Five hundred in gold for your wavy locks."

"A thousand, I might think about it," Pappy chuckled. "That Snake River Valley is some kind of cattle and horse country. Grass this high, plenty of sweet water, and the Indians ain't always lookin' for your scalp. I've heard of this Bronco Johnny. Be a mean one and a back shooter."

"That's him. Well, he ain't the first to want me dead. Get the word out that I killed Pepper. Maybe that'll bring him to me and we'll get it over with. We're off, Wild Bill. Hope to see you again soon."

Corcoran groaned loud getting himself into the saddle amid Pappy's loud laughter, and joshing from Kick about a little bruise or two, and they rode out on the well-travelled emigrant trail for Elko. It was a cool fall day with lots of sunshine, little wind, and the packs on the mule were full. Neither man looked back as they crossed the tracks out of town.

That old town's in better shape that when we got here, and I can't say the same thing for me. So, Bronco Johnny Ladd is after my hide, eh? Well, buster, a lot better men than you have tried, and none of them are around to tell you just how I took them out of the picture. I'm gonna miss you, Miss Bonét.

It was the following morning that found George Anders in the blacksmith's stables finishing tying off the packs on the mule. "You tie a good knot, son," the stable man said looking over the pack. "You folks stirred up the dust while you were here, but looks like it'll be quiet now for some time. Gotta say, I didn't have many good thoughts about Dean Whitaker or Humboldt Charley."

"I guess there will always be those that don't care much

for the law or the people they hurt." George Anders said. He had turned in his badge that morning, telling Sheriff Kick that he would be working full time at the Moss ranch. "You're right, though, old timer. This little town will be better off with Whitaker and his lot gone."

Jeanne Moss walked in with a smile seeing the mule all packed and ready. She brought that fine gelding out of its stall and saddled up. Anders had his ready to saddle and their long journey was about to begin.

"A nice day for a long ride, eh Mr. Anders?"

"It is that, my lovely lady. We'll camp outside Halleck and make Elko tomorrow. I missed saying goodbye to Corcoran and Pappy."

"They left yesterday, George. Terrence stopped by and said Pappy would wait for us in Eureka. He wants to ride back with us."

"Good. I like riding with that old man. There isn't a minute on the trail that I don't learn something from him." He gathered up his reins along with the mule's lead rope, and they headed out of Wells. It was going to be a long journey, Anders thought. *Might take sixty years or more for this journey of ours.*

"I want you to start with the corner post on the nearest corral and tell me everything about the Moss ranch and the Monitor Valley." Anders carried a broad smile on his young face, as did Jeanne Moss. "And when you're through with that, I want to know everything there is to know about the Moss family."

"That's fair, George Anders, and when I'm through, there will be plenty of time for you to tell me everything about this Anders family I'm about to become a part of."

It would be a long and wonderful ride, this ride through life the two were beginning.

A LOOK AT RAGE ON THE RANGE (TERRENCE CORCORAN BOOK III)

Corcoran takes some time off as Eureka County Deputy Sheriff to visit an old family friend and stumbles into a land fraud scheme. It gets mighty dangerous as a conspiracy develops, one layer at a time, and bodies begin to pile up. A rancher leaves his foreman in charge in order to get medical help for his daughter and the foreman claims the man abandoned his homestead claim.

Corcoran being Corcoran, he meets a charming young lady whose father is an Oregon County Sheriff. He seriously contemplates giving up his badge and settling down.

AVAILABLE NOW.

ABOUT THE AUTHOR

Reno, Nevada novelist, Johnny Gunn, is retired from a long career in journalism. He has worked in print, broadcast, and Internet, including a stint as publisher and editor of the Virginia City Legend. These days, Gunn spends most of his time writing novel length fiction, concentrating on the western genre. Or, you can find him down by the Truckee River with a fly rod in hand.

"it's been a wonderful life. I was born in Santa Cruz, California, on the north shore of fabled Monterey Bay. When I was fourteen, that would have been 1953, we moved to Guam and I went through my high school years living in a tropical paradise. I learned to scuba dive from a WWII Navy Frogman, learned to fly from a WWII combat pilot (by dad), but I knew how to fish long before I moved to Guam.

"I spent time on the Island of Truk, which during WWII was a huge Japanese naval base, and dived in the lagoon. Massive U.S. air strikes sunk thousands of tons of Japanese naval craft, and it was more than exciting to dive on those wrecks. In the Palau Islands, near Koror, I also dived on Japanese aircraft that had been shot down into the lagoons.

https://wolfpackpublishing.com/johnny-gunn/